SEMINAR
FOR
MURDER

SEMINAR FOR MURDER

B.M.Gill

CHARLES SCRIBNER'S SONS
NEW YORK

First published in the United States by Charles Scribner's Sons 1986.
Copyright © 1985 B. M. Gill

Library of Congress Cataloging-in-Publication Data

Gill, B. M.
    Seminar for murder.

    I. Title.
PR6057.I538S4   1986   823'.914   85-24986
ISBN 0-684-18651-9

1 3 5 7 9 11 13 15 17 19   F/C   20 18 16 14 12 10 8 6 4 2

Printed in the United States of America.

SEMINAR
FOR
MURDER

Chapter ONE

Detective Chief Inspector Tom Maybridge was not gifted with second sight. If he had been, he would have refused to lecture at the crime writers' seminar. He would have stayed at home and tended his garden and not become embroiled in the bizarre series of events that were not only horrific but also personally very embarrassing.

However, on this bright autumn Saturday, with no premonition of disaster to trouble him, his mood was tranquil. His lecture to the members of the Golden Guillotine Club wasn't due to be delivered until two-thirty, and so he decided to drive the longer, more picturesque route across the Downs.

Here, within close proximity of the busy center of Bristol but not within sight of it, the eighteenth-century terraces, elegant and charming, had the peaceful aura of a time long gone. The open grasslands, thick in places with bronze and crimson trees, trailed their colors like ancient tapestries. The Clifton Suspension Bridge, bone white over olive-green water, was easy on the eye.

And easy for suicides.

Maybridge's mood became less content as present-day problems began to obtrude. All large cities were stressful. One day, when he retired, he mused, he'd buy himself a small-holding in the Cotswolds. He would distance himself totally from police work—all sight, sound, and smell of it. He would grow roses and keep bees and read farming manuals.

It was extraordinary how fascinated the layman could be with books about death at its most sordid. He glanced at the box of forensic slides on the seat beside him. Perhaps he should have weeded out the worst of them. They weren't pleasant. Some were shocking. The writers he was going to show them to weren't hardened by experience; they were men and women with macabre imaginations who made loot out of other people's vicarious fascination with murder. A good deal of loot—some of them. It was rumored that Sir Godfrey Grant, the chairman and founder of the Golden Guillotine Club, owned an Elizabethan manor in Wiltshire, a villa in Portugal, and most probably, a bank account in Switzerland. What hardworking chief inspector could ever aspire to that?

He had met Grant at the local golf links and played a few rounds with him. Between holes they had discussed hybrid tea roses, Maybridge's specialty, and later, over drinks at the clubhouse, Grant had asked his opinion about a couple of police procedural novels that had recently been published. Maybridge hadn't read them but commented on the kind of details that crime writers often got wrong. The following week, the invitation to the seminar had arrived. Grant's note, pinned to the weekend program, had been scrawled with a black ballpoint pen. "We'd be delighted if you'd come along. A retired police officer from London was due to give a talk on ballistics, but he's been laid low by appendicitis. If you could fill the gap, we'd be more than grateful," it urged hopefully. "It's a small club—just thirty writers. We meet annually, and from a short list of six books by our members, vote for the winner of the Golden Guillotine Award. The venue is the university hall of residence, St. Quentin's. We have the use of it from Friday to Sunday evening. The food isn't bad, and I'll personally supervise the booze. The accommodation is in single rooms if you'd like to stay Saturday night, following the dinner and presentation of the award."

Perhaps Maybridge wouldn't have accepted if his wife, an English don at Bristol University, hadn't been going to America for six weeks to lecture on Restoration prose. But in her absence, preparing to present his own less erudite subject matter gave him something to think about. Sir Godfrey had suggested that he might like to drive over before lunch and sit in on the morning lectures, though Maybridge, interpreting this as an invitation to see how it should be done, politely declined. Being in the company of an assorted bunch of authors all through a Saturday afternoon and evening was long enough. He half regretted saying that he would also sleep in the building that night, but with Meg away, the house was lonely.

St. Quentin's was a large Victorian mansion on a tree-lined avenue not far from the local shopping area. Here the view was less rural, less beautiful; the city began to intrude. Turning in at the gates, he drove the Peugeot up to the wide semicircular graveled area where a dozen cars were already parked.

He had expected to be met by Grant but instead was greeted by a middle-aged man with dyed brown hair who introduced himself as Dwight Connors and then apologized profusely for Grant's temporary absence.

He offered to help unload the car. "I believe you have a portable screen and projector?"

Maybridge nodded, and they each took one end of the screen, with Maybridge carrying the projector and slides in his free hand.

St. Quentin's was old and shabby and badly modernized in places, but here on the ground floor it had retained its dignity. Connors took him through the wide, drafty corridor to the lecture hall, an imposing and beautifully proportioned room with a high ceiling and ornate cornices. Maybridge looked around him appreciatively as he followed Connors up to the stage, made bright by book jackets pinned to a display screen.

"Do you write crime novels, too?" he asked.

"Heaven forfend," Connors said in unconscious imitation of Grant at his most pompous.

"They looked reasonably normal to me," Maybridge observed, referring to the group of writers they had passed on their way to the lecture room.

"Don't be deceived." Connors grinned. He examined the plug on the projector, and taking out a small screwdriver from the pocket of his jeans, tightened it.

"What are you?" Maybridge asked, approving of him. "An electrician?"

"Among other things. General factotum—researcher. You name it, I do it."

"Grant's personal secretary?"

"And literary agent. I roam foreign fields with Grant's literary output."

For twenty percent? Maybridge wondered. If so, this man could be on to a good thing.

Connors pushed the plug into a socket at the side of the stage and tried the projector. It worked. He asked Maybridge if he had read any of the books that had been nominated for the award.

"Sir Godfrey sent them to me when I agreed to give the lecture. Ploughing through them took me the best part of ten days."

"Ploughing denotes rather cloddy earth," Connors warned. "It's a verb writers don't like."

"Tough"—Maybridge smiled—"but I'll do my best not to use it." He told Connors that he had read Grant's latest book, *The Helius Factor*, and wondered why it wasn't in competition for the award with the others.

"The Guillotine," Connors explained, "is an annual gift

made by Grant himself. It's eighteen-carat gold and worth a few hundred. To give with one hand and claw back with the other would rather tarnish the image." The remark was caustic and perhaps unwise. But before Maybridge could respond, Connors left him and went backstage to fetch a green baize table. When he returned, he suggested to the chief inspector that he should put the projector on top of it. "You'll find it's the right height." He helped Maybridge set it up and wished him luck with his lecture. Connors wondered how this policeman would make out. Better than the other one, he sensed. Last year's speaker, Inspector Grimshaw, perhaps already plagued by a grumbling appendix, had been dull and rather nervous, whereas Maybridge gave the impression of a general strategically placed on top of a hill, waiting with some amusement for the approaching enemy. Connors told him where he'd find his bedroom. "Names have been taped to the door. I think you've been put next to a new club member, Scott Wilson. Bathrooms and lavatories are at the end of the corridor. In term time, students live here, so the accommodation is spartan but adequate."

Maybridge, unpacking his pajamas a little later, agreed with the description. It reminded him of the police college he had attended some years ago, if marginally more comfortable. The narrow bed faced a window that obviously extended into the bedroom next door. The partition wall, painted green, was flimsy and wouldn't be sound-proof. He hoped his neighbor wasn't a transistor addict. Someone had left a full box of tissues on the bedside cabinet. It occurred to him that a financial empire could be built more easily by producing blank paper that was disposable than by writing books—a heretical thought in the present circumstances. Smiling, Maybridge took his scribbled notes out of the inner pocket of his fawn sports jacket and glanced through them. The early part of the lecture would tread familiar ground—guns, and murder in its unpleasant reality. The second part was about fictional corpses amazingly and erroneously done to death. Humming happily, he settled down to underline some of the more glaring examples.

Ten minutes before Maybridge's lecture was due to start, Sir Godfrey walked into the lecture room with his wife, Fay, at his side. It had been a traumatic morning, preceded by a busy week of preparation for the seminar. And today, when everything appeared to be going smoothly at last, Bonny Harper had arrived with her bastard infant. "And Godfrey's word was made flesh," Bonny had taunted him in the ensuing row, "and his name is Ulysses."

It had taken Sir Godfrey some time to subdue his anger. A small scotch had helped. A large one would have helped more, but he was diabetic and had to go easy. Bonny's periodic demands for maintenance were usually made by letter; this was the first time he had actually seen the child. There was no doubt that it was his. He glanced at the dust jacket of Bonny's book, which was pinned up with the others on the stage—a winter scene in orange and umber with a small wraithlike corpse lying like mist in the marsh—and couldn't help wishing bitterly that it was a photograph of Bonny herself after rigor mortis had set in.

Maybridge, aware of tensions he didn't understand, shook hands with Fay. He had heard she was Eurasian—half Indian, half Scottish. An improbable mixture. Sir Godfrey's second wife and his former secretary, she was several years younger than her husband. Sir Godfrey, however, though in his middle forties, looked his vigorous best. So immaculate, he seemed freshly minted, whereas Fay looked as if she had come out of a hot kitchen. Her dress, plain and very expensive cream linen, didn't suit her. She should wear bright colors, Maybridge thought, even the ethnic stuff some of the youngsters went in for. He tried to imagine her in a sari and failed. She was big and clumsy and had a rawboned beauty that was totally Scottish. Only her dark eyes and glossy black hair, held insecurely with a tortoiseshell comb, showed her Indian origins. She apologized for not having been there to greet him when he arrived.

"Everything working?" Sir Godfrey asked, referring to the projector.

Maybridge said it was.

"There's nothing I can do to assist you?"

Maybridge, puzzled by his rather distrait manner, told him there wasn't.

"Then I'll just stay on stage to introduce you. After that, it's all yours."

Maybridge looked at the slowly filling lecture room with interest. They came in all shapes and sizes, this unknown breed. He imagined them plotting at their typewriters, dreaming of murder and mayhem. One of them, he noticed, was quite elderly. Her hair was white, and she wore a gray two-piece with pearls—real, cultured, fake? Apparently you could make nothing, something, or a lot in this profession. The old lady had brought her knitting. Shades of Miss Marple?

Cora Larsbury caught the inspector's glance and smiled. He smiled back. Pleasant man, she thought. Nasty job. Research for her last novel had taken her to Egypt, to the Valley of the Kings. There had been massive granite heads lying in the sand. Very impressive heads. His was an impressive head. Strong, though not handsome. Pity he was developing a paunch. And his legs were rather short. The headless Egyptian kings had sat stiffly, hands on muscular knees. Who had vandalized them? she wondered. The implacable march of time, no doubt. Time had a lot to answer for.

It hadn't been very tactful of Fay to have mentioned her seventieth birthday. A very special birthday, Fay had said. What would she like for it? Cora had nearly replied, "Publication of my new book," but that would have been too much like probing for Sir Godfrey's reaction to it. He had received

the manuscript a fortnight ago and had had ample time to
read it and discuss it with Fay. He was sure to be critical of
some aspects of it, but his criticism was constructive and
courteous, and she always took notice of what he had to say.
She was usually optimistic about all her books but sensed with
this one that she had created something extra special. With a
little guidance from Sir Godfrey, it could well crash the barrier
and make it into print. It was heartening that someone so
influential in the book world should pay her the respect of
serious attention. Earlier that afternoon, in the novice seminar,
she had warned the new young man, Scott Wilson, to be re-
ceptive to whatever Sir Godfrey had to tell him. "After all,"
she had said, "you are here to learn."

"I'm a fallow field," he had replied cheerfully, "ready to
be sown with mind-boggling success."

As if telepathically, Maybridge's glance left Cora Larsbury
and turned to the object of Cora's thoughts. A young husband
and wife team plus child, Maybridge conjectured, mildly surprised to see a baby in the room. But Bonny and Scott had only
recently met at the midday lecture. Scott had commented that
Ulysses was a smashing kid. "But for Christ's sake, why give
him a name like that?" Was Bonny an admirer of James
Joyce? Bonny had told him that Gen. Ulysses Grant, one-time
president of the United States, was a forebear of the child's
appalling dad. The explanation had delighted Scott, and now
he and Ulysses were conversing together very happily.

When Maybridge had given lectures in the past, to the
police, the setting had always been formal. He preferred it
that way. Here all the chairs were grouped in untidy semi-
circles. If anyone got bored, all he had to do was to turn his
chair the other way and go to sleep—or walk out. The room
was almost full now, and most of the chairs were occupied.
Maybridge, very much on his mettle, checked the slides once
more and nodded that he was ready.

Sir Godfrey walked to the center of the stage and waited

for silence. The last sound to die away proved to be a hiccup from Ulysses. Father and son regarded each other malevolently. It hadn't occurred to Sir Godfrey that Bonny would bring the child to the lecture room. Dwight should have stopped her. The seminars of previous years had been pleasant affairs. This one was not, and all it needed now was for the chief inspector to make a mess of his lecture to put the finishing touches on a thoroughly trying day.

"It gives me very great pleasure," Sir Godfrey said predictably, "to introduce Detective Chief Inspector Maybridge to you. As you'll remember, in previous years our lecturer was Inspector Grimshaw of the metropolitan police. He's unable to be with us this year, but we're extremely fortunate that the chief inspector has agreed to fill the breach. . . ." He smiled. "If you'll forgive the pun—with bullets. His topic is ballistics."

It was a clumsy quip, and no one responded. Sir Godfrey paused for a few seconds, momentarily disconcerted, then went on. "If the chief inspector later in his talk aims a verbal bullet or two in the way of criticism in your direction, you must bear with him and be grateful. We may be crime writers, but we are not crime experts." He stepped back from center stage. "Please welcome Chief Inspector Maybridge, who will entertain us with a seminar on murder."

Chapter TWO

Maybridge waited for the polite applause to stop. "Any verbal bullets I may fire," he said pleasantly, "won't be discharged with lethal intent. However, if you feel the need to withdraw from range and are not quite sure where that might be, then let me remind you." So far so good; the audience seemed scrupulously attentive. Maybridge pressed on.

"A near discharge is within arm's reach. A distant discharge by pistol is about five hundred yards. A rifle can fire effectively up to three thousand yards. As your common room is safely around the corner, some of you might like to take flight before I begin. My lecture won't be cozy, but I hope it won't be dull, either. About half the slides I'm going to show you are about the workings of firearms. You should all be *au fait* with the mechanisms of different types. The information will be technical, but I promise to be brief. What you need to know, if you write descriptively, is the effect of the bullet on the human body. Entry and exit wounds and so on. The slides aren't pretty but are nevertheless very necessary for crime detection. If you have no stomach for them, then your chairs are conveniently arranged so that you may turn your backs. You write very tough books, ladies and gentlemen, but painting blood on a canvas is a long way removed from looking at the real thing. I hope that by the end of the lecture you will all be with me, but it will certainly be no sign of weakness if you are not." He folded his arms and looked at his audience. Slightly nervous, everyone looked back. Ulysses snuggled down in Bonny's arms and stuck his thumb in his mouth. His eyelids closed sleepily.

"He'll have seen worse on the telly," Scott whispered to Bonny. "Anyway, at his age it won't mean a thing."

Bonny hoped he was right. She could easily have left Ulysses in the care of a neighbor, but it was time he saw his father and—more importantly—time his father saw him. She had a sudden vivid memory of Ulysses in the garden of her North London flat. The flat was small and damp and lacked light, but the garden was a glorious wilderness filled with rioting bushes and long, lush grass. In the middle of it stood a gnarled walnut tree. This year there was an abundance of nuts and an abundance of squirrels eating them. Ulysses, last Saturday afternoon—a week today, in fact—had been sitting in his pram chortling at the squirrels. A butterfly alighted on his blue-mittened hand. He raised his hand carefully. It trembled on his fingertips, and then, in a flutter of red and orange, it took off. He had watched it solemnly, and then he had turned and smiled at her.

She held him closer. Fighting Godfrey on his behalf was a nasty business. Ballistics, not butterflies, she reminded herself.

Maybridge asked for the curtains to be drawn so that the slides could come into sharper focus. Major Lawrence Haydon, near one of the side windows, stepped carefully around his dog Marcus and pulled the heavy green velvet. Marcus thumped his tail in recognition of his master. "Good dog," Haydon whispered. So far he had avoided an encounter with Sir Godfrey Grant. The man knew the golden retriever was there, of course; he had seen them arrive. Grant's displeasure at the dog's presence had cut across the room like a laser beam. Haydon returned to the chair next to his son, Christopher, who was sitting with stiffly folded arms, staring absolutely ahead.

So far, Maybridge thought. I still have their attention. And if I can get over to them the mechanics of ballistics as quickly as possible, I'll keep it. He turned to the screen; the slides at this stage were diagrammatic. "Lock, stock, and barrel," he said, "a common term we all know—add breech and extractor and you've got a rifle." He went on. "Rifled weapons are either long barreled or short barreled; short barreled rifles are pistols. There is a considerable difference in breech pressure. In a rifle, it can be up to about twenty tons; in a pistol, about four to six tons. Imagine the impact on flesh and bone. The two common types of pistol are the revolver—which has a revolving chamber—and the automatic, fashioned to use clips of bullets." He showed them slides of the different loading mechanisms.

"Now we move on to slides depicting actual cases. Let me rephrase that. They're about people. Dead people. Tragically and nastily dead, be it by murder or suicide. All this is your stock-in-trade. And mine. But you skim the surface, ladies and gentlemen; I don't. By that, I hope I'm not patronizing you. I don't mean to. I couldn't write a book. I haven't your expertise. But you couldn't solve a murder. You're brilliant bluffers and work to make death an entertainment. It isn't."

The purpose of this part of his lecture was to show how to differentiate between murder and suicide. A bullet discharged through the mouth, blowing off the cranial vault, didn't leave much room for doubt. A bullet through the heart sometimes did, and he showed them both. The next slide was of a contact wound made by a suicide using a twelve-bore shotgun. He compared it with a discharge from a similar gun at twenty yards. "Shot spread over twenty inches indicates that the range was about twenty yards. Obviously murder."

The next half-dozen slides were similar, and he invited

comment from the audience. "Bear in mind that the dispersal of the shot depends on the choking of the bore, so it's an approximation. However, a suicide is limited by the length of his arms. What would you say to these—suicide or murder?" The answers were murmured hesitantly; some of the slides were distinctly unpleasant.

Feeling slightly guilty, Maybridge remembered the elderly lady and looked over in her direction. She was still knitting in the half-light and seemed perfectly composed. The baby on the young mother's knee was asleep. Maybridge wasn't concerned about anybody else.

"Now," he continued confidently, "bullet wounds not shotgun wounds. Deciding the range here is more difficult." He explained about lateral waves of pressure having a tearing effect on the flesh. "The range may be defined up to about eighty yards with a pistol and about two hundred yards with a rifle. All this is textbook stuff, and you'll need to do a lot more background reading if you want to write about it in any depth."

Maybridge then went on to list and show the elective sites for suicides—the temple, the heart, the roof of the mouth, the forehead. "A murderer might shoot his victim in the face, below the forehead; but I have yet to see a suicide do so. There's a psychological aversion to certain sites. If you have a corpse in your book and he's been shot through the eye, then either it's an accident, or it's murder." He smiled. "But don't take my word for it, of course. Your corpses are your own. Quite splendid ones, too, some of them. And if I had half the intelligence and luck of some of your detectives, I would have been made a commissioner years ago."

He looked down into the audience and noticed that Fay was sitting with her eyes closed. She opened them cautiously, wondering why Maybridge had paused. "Those of you who don't write," he said, "have suffered my talk very stoically. Those of you who do, and whose books I've read and intend

talking about, will, I hope, suffer my comments with equal
stoicism. Please remember, I couldn't do it at all. Any of it."

He emptied the projector and turned it so that the light
beamed onto the book jackets pinned to the display screen.

"I believe these are the books that are in competition for
the Golden Guillotine Award." He addressed Grant, who had
gone down into the audience and was sitting next to Fay.
"Have you taken the final count yet, Sir Godfrey?"

Grant said that the thirty members of the club had put their
votes in sealed envelopes. The votes would be counted that
evening just before the presentation.

"So anything I say won't influence the result in any way?"

"To no degree," Grant assured him. And thankful that his
his own book wasn't in competition with the rest, he settled
himself back in his chair in happy anticipation.

Maybridge went over to the display board and pointed to
the dust jacket pinned to the far left. "The time factor," he
said, "plays rather an important part of *Death Is Discreet*. I
wonder if the author was thinking of the Haigh case when he
wrote this? Is Mr. Trevor Martin with us?"

The author was indeed present, though he couldn't help
wishing that he was not. Trevor Martin was a forty-three-
year-old arts master at a large comprehensive school, though
a chemistry degree might have served his writing rather better.
Certainly he had trodden gingerly on unknown territory.

He stood up. "I'm here. And yes, I did base it on the Haigh
case. In what way was I wrong?"

"Your error was no greater than Haigh's," Maybridge commented, "but it cost him his neck. He used sulfuric acid to dispose of his corpse. So did you. He couldn't dispose of her
dentures. Neither could you. I take it you didn't want to?"

"For the purpose of the story," said Trevor Martin, "no."

"Quite," said Maybridge. "But if you wanted the discretion
to be total, and I do realize it would have spoiled the yarn,

then a further period of immersion in the acid would have got rid of the teeth together with the acrylic gum base."

"I of course knew this," said Martin, whose flush betrayed him.

"Then I beg your pardon for pointing it out," Maybridge retorted diplomatically. "It's just a scrap of information that might be useful for someone else."

"We're indebted," Martin said, sitting down.

Good Lord, Maybridge thought. He minded!

"The application of the science of finger printing occurs in nearly all the books. You've obviously done some reading on this, and most of it is right. The Chester Barrington book *Count Four, Then Fire!* centers around the inability to finger-print the corpse. A little further reading would have shown you that the superintendent gave up too easily on this one. Which of you is Chester Barrington?"

Kate and Lloyd Cooper stood up, and Maybridge saw that Lloyd was wearing a peculiar hood. That he could bear being the focus of attention was a tribute to the expertise of the plastic surgeons and his psychiatrist, but mainly to the loving care of his wife. The fire in the Swiss hotel had occurred three years before, on their tenth wedding anniversary. Kate had escaped unscathed. Lloyd, foolishly, had returned for a partially drafted typescript. Nowadays, after intensive hospital treatment followed by more minor surgery, he was learning to go among people again and not mind. Or not mind too much. The hood hid the worst of his disfigurement, and he resisted touching it as he answered Maybridge's question.

"We're a writing team," he explained. "My wife, Kate, and I."

Maybridge's lecture had amused him. The chief inspector had put it across well. He was rather like a matador prancing among the bulls. Literary wounds were minor scars when placed in perspective.

He expanded his answer. "We're Lloyd and Kate Cooper. I was born in Chester. Kate's hometown was Warrington. Chester Warrington sounded too much like a railway time-table, so Warrington became Barrington."

"An effective pseudonym," Maybridge said quietly. The reason why the tall man with the pleasant speaking voice was wearing the headgear had suddenly occurred to him. Total recall of a sentence in Sir Godfrey Grant's book *The Helius Factor* came to him. "The hideous scarring resembled a child's effort to clobber together a human head out of clay; in order to be acceptable to public view, Manders wore a knitted hood lined with gray silk." The rest of the paragraph returned to him in fragments: "psychologically a walking disaster," "narcissistically twisted and overaware," "obsessed by his wounds, unable to think beyond them." Pompous, but vitriolic stuff nevertheless.

Maybridge looked over at Sir Godfrey, who sat examining his carefully manicured fingernails. A deliberate description? Maybridge wondered. Could anyone set out to be so cruel? If the answer was yes, why was Lloyd Cooper here? Obviously, if his wounds were anything like those described by Grant, he wouldn't be. Nobody could be that masochistic, or forgiving. A bad case of alopecia, perhaps; or shingles—surely nothing more? He had obviously jumped to the wrong conclusion. Maybridge did a quick rethink, absolved Grant—at least temporarily—and returned to the topic of conversation.

"I enjoyed the book," he said. "In fact, I enjoyed all of them."

"Thank you," said Kate, contributing to the partnership for the first time.

She was the same age as her husband, Maybridge guessed, in her middle thirties. Her face, with its wide cheekbones and well-defined chin, had character rather than beauty. Her voice was strong and carried none of the undertones of amusement he had detected in the man's. In a writing partnership, he supposed, someone had to dominate.

"Your corpse had been dead for some time," he said. "Decomposition had set in. However, the fact that the fingers were rotting didn't preclude the possibility of a print being taken. In cases like this, reversal photography can be used. I think your murderer would have been found a great deal earlier if the forensic team knew just a few more basic facts of detection."

"A book needs to run to a reasonable length," Lloyd pointed out mildly, "but thanks, anyway."

Maybridge was glad that he had taken it so well. "And there's one other detail—a point of law. Your book isn't set in Scotland, is it?"

"No," Kate and Lloyd answered together.

"Pity, because if it had been, your method of treating the major suspect—I've forgotten his name—would have been correct."

"Lerwick Masterton," Lloyd reminded him, "and we hoped it would be memorable." He was smiling.

Maybridge smiled back. "Yes, well, all these books in a short space of time took some getting through. Anyway, Lerwick Masterton wouldn't have been fingerprinted in England without his permission unless he had been convicted or authority to do so had been obtained from a magistrate to whom the police inspector would have applied. In Scotland he would have been fingerprinted on arrest whether he gave permission or not."

"Thanks again," said Lloyd.

Kate and Lloyd were a pleasant couple, Maybridge thought as they sat down.

"The novel I want to talk about now is forensically so accurate that I'm overcome with admiration." He beamed the spotlight on the dust jacket of *Kill Me a Scorpion*. "Quite a lot

of you think that rigor mortis goes on forever—I suppose
that's why corpses are called stiffs. The author of this novel
has written an excellent paragraph detailing the changes in
the body when rigor first appears—in five to seven hours, until
it is fully established at twelve to eighteen hours—and then
goes on to describe how it passes away in the following twenty-
four to thirty-six hours. Not only does she do this quite
faultlessly, with the corpse found in the attic of the boarding
house, she also describes the less exact onset of rigor in the
corpse found in the waterlogged cellar. In this case—correctly
—the rigor went on for four days. A very good piece of research work, Miss Muriel Slocombe. I hope you're here, too."

For a half minute or so, nobody stirred. Then, very reluctantly, a thickset bearded man at the back of the hall slowly
rose to his feet.

Maybridge looked at him in astonishment. Even in the
dim light it would be impossible not to recognize Dr. Sandy
Crofton. He was reputed to be one of the most able cardi-
ologists in the South West and was also well known in the
city as a fund raiser for the Bristol Infirmary. The doctor was
the first to recover his equilibrium. "Oh, to be Miss Slocombe," he said, "now that Maybridge is here. Your praise
makes my heart flutter, sir. Under my beard I blush like a
rose."

The audience tittered, perhaps relieved that Maybridge
had found something to praise at last.

"But if anyone blabs outside this room that I am a she—
or a disguised he—I shall personally rip out his heart and
transplant it in a baboon." His mock ferocity covered a very
real annoyance. He had expected Maybridge's talk to be
more general and without reference to individual authors.
His fellow club members knew his identity, of course—that
was inevitable—but they didn't divulge it. And his books
made money for the hospital. Only under the cloak of ano-
nymity could he write them. Murder and surgical skill might

go very well together, but not in the eyes of a patient or the hospital board.

Maybridge, delighted that life could still offer moments of gut-thumping humor, let his powerful deep belly laugh boom out. He was glad he had come. He was *very* glad he had come. How had Crofton managed to keep Mrs. Hyde separate from Dr. Jekyll for so long? he thought. Just wait until Meg came home so that he could tell her about it. No one else, of course.

"I can assure you," he said, "that I don't intend benefiting any baboon."

"Good," said Crofton. "I'm relieved that the hospital can continue to receive small gifts from macabre sources." He grimaced. "Now that you have sugared the pill with kind words about my forensic accuracy, you're going to make me swallow something rather bitter? In what way is *Kill Me a Scorpion* drastically wrong?"

"Well," said Maybridge, enjoying himself more and more, "if I had been the murderer and wanted to kill um, er—"

"Dodson," Crofton supplied helpfully.

"I would have boarded the train and dispatched him in the railway carriage. I wouldn't have waited in a car at the level crossing, particularly as the train slowed but didn't stop."

"Then you would have been nicked," Crofton pointed out.

"My chance of getting out of the train as it slowed would have been a great deal better than the murderer's chance of killing Dodson. Unless your murderer has a mind like Pythagoras."

"I suppose," Crofton ventured, "that you're now going to lecture me on the line of trajectory—bullets in flight, tail wag, and so on. I mugged up on it and didn't understand a word."

Maybridge indicated a pile of neatly Xeroxed notes on

the table by the projector. "Then make sure you take one of
these information sheets at the end of the afternoon. They'll
tell you how it should be done. Was the carriage window
open or closed, by the way?"

"Oh, most definitely open," Crofton said.

"Then, as we're talking of the modern railway carriage,
the victim must have been standing up so that his forehead
was neatly framed in a small rectangle at the precise moment
the murderer fired—telepathic control?"

"Bloody luck," Crofton said amiably.

But Maybridge had made a fool of him, and it rankled a
little. It was small consolation that he would probably make
fools of them all before long.

Maybridge's criticism of *Death at Daybreak* was less
humorous. It was an unpleasant book about suicide by hang-
ing. The author, B. R. Anderson, a gentle-looking man in his
sixties, heard him out politely. Or perhaps he didn't hear
him. The way he inclined his head led Maybridge to believe
that he was deaf. "Your victim," he told him, "with such a
short drop, would have died from asphyxia, not a broken
neck. According to weight, the drop should have been at
least six and a half feet to seven and a half feet. The neck
has to be jerked in order to cause a separation fracture of
the cervical segments. It wouldn't have jerked at only three
feet."

"Oh, yes, quite," Anderson said slowly. He took out a large
white linen handkerchief and blew his nose.

Maybridge waited until he had put the handkerchief back
in his pocket. "Apart from that," he said, "it was carefully
researched." He didn't add that it was the only one that had
depressed him. But then suicide always had.

Transfer to Death was probably the most literary offering
of the lot. Maybridge didn't know much about style, but
obviously Lawrence Haydon had sufficient expertise to make
the story credible.

"I liked it," he told him honestly. "While I was reading it, I believed in it."

The elderly retired major stood stiffly at attention, next to his dog. "But now you think it's a load of old rope," the major suggested brusquely.

"A rather peculiar theme, well handled," Maybridge ventured cautiously.

"An old and well-worn theme," Major Haydon said. "Lots of different versions. You mentioned Pythagoras just now—he believed in transmigration. So had Empedocles, another Greek philosopher. Several religious sects believed in different versions. In my yarn, the souls changed place in life. Not possession—a straight switch. If you want to criticize it as codswallop, then do."

"I don't," Maybridge protested, sensing heavy anger tightly controlled.

"But there's something the matter with it?"

"Only that the adolescent girl with the soul of the murderer didn't know much about strychnine. The victim would have suffered several seizures—characterized by arching of the back —and then finally died of exhaustion. I'm not a forensic expert, but I'm fairly sure you described poisoning by aconite."

"The nun in my book and used aconite." Sir Godfrey's voice, though not loud, was clear. He half turned in his chair and looked at Haydon across the lecture room. Fay hastily put her hand on his. Maybridge saw the warning gesture.

Lawrence Haydon had heard. "Damn your nun," the old man said crisply. "I haven't read your puerile story. Anyway, aconite—strychnine—what does it matter?"

"Whether it matters or not," Grant said, "this isn't the place to discuss it." He was as tense as Haydon but managed not to show it.

"And why not?" Young Christopher Haydon was on his feet now. "You accused my father of plagiarism in an open letter in the club bulletin— Oh, not in so many words, but

the innuendo was plain. Add slander to libel—loud and clear.
Come on; let's hear it!" He was shaking with rage.

Sir Godfrey turned away from both father and son with a
dismissive gesture and addressed himself to Maybridge. "I
think it might be better, inspector, if you went on to the next
book."

Maybridge agreed with him. The air was thick with hatred.
He had inadvertently stirred up a hornet's nest and couldn't
get out of it quickly enough.

He spoke coolly and levelly. "Let me just say once again
how much I enjoyed the book," he told Haydon. "I shall look
out for your other novels." He hoped that the injured party
would accept the honestly spoken compliment and sit down
peacefully. The major, after a moment's hesitation, did so, and
Christopher reluctantly followed suit.

Maybridge turned with some relief to *Murder in the Marsh*.
It was bad; it was silly. But it was also funny. "A very nice
dust jacket," he said. "Who wrote this one?"

Bonny put the sleeping Ulysses on Scott Wilson's knee. "I
did," she said, standing up.

"A single-handed effort?" Maybridge asked, "or are you and
your husband a writing team, too?"

"Christ!" Bonny said, getting the drift. "I'm not married to
him. I'm not married, period. She looked at the back of Sir
Godfrey's head and then glanced at Scott, who grinned at her.
Ulysses was nuzzling up against him like a puppy between the
paws of a Saint Bernard. "I write my own books," Bonny said,
"without help from anybody."

"Excellent," Maybridge replied. But it was a polite comment; she was a pretty woman. The baby, he supposed, was
hers. Born out of wedlock, like a great many more; or perhaps
she was looking after it for somebody else. Anyway, it had
nothing to do with the book.

"Your Stephanie Lawless is quite a character," he said.

"She lurks inside my subconscious like a lioness in its lair."

"A very intuitive lioness."

"Fast, sleek, beautiful, and brainy." Bonny smiled. "With long sharp claws."

Maybridge didn't agree with "brainy" but liked Bonny too well to say so. He wondered if the very large young man holding the baby was its father. They presented a nice domestic group, the three of them.

"But your lioness occasionally takes leaps in the wrong direction," he observed gently. "A great many supersleuths do the same."

"They're called red herrings," Bonny pointed out, aware that metaphors were becoming mixed. She was also aware that Maybridge was about to say something derogatory about the skill of Stephanie Lawless and was seeking some tactful words in which to clothe the criticism.

"Well, yes, I know," said Maybridge. "You scattered your red herrings very well and deceived me for most of the time, but there is one major point . . ." He hesitated.

"My ego might be rather sensitive," Bonny said, "but if you wound me, I won't throw a tantrum."

"It's just that your victim—Carlos, wasn't it, the Spaniard? —is found dead in a pool in the center of the marsh."

"Lying in four feet of water, held by reeds, his face obscured by water lilies," Bonny supplied helpfully.

"But before being put in the water, he had been asphyxiated."

"An ether-soaked rag applied by the murderer in the back of his car. A Porsche," Bonny added. She liked cars. Stephanie Lawless drove a Lamborghini.

"After he was asphyxiated, the murderer put him in the pool to give the impression of drowning," Maybridge recapped. "There was an autopsy, and the verdict was accidental death by drowning."

"Yes, that was the way it looked. He had been drinking. There was a mist. He had slipped. Only, of course, he hadn't."

"Had the pathologist who performed the post mortem been drinking, too?"

"You are about to fell me with a lethal blow," Bonny said calmly. "I suggest you get it over with fast."

Maybridge did, and as kindly as possible. "When a living body is drowned, there are certain classical changes, including a ballooning of the lungs. The inhaled water becomes a fine froth and is found in the terminal air passages. In your book, the victim was dead when he was immersed. The water wouldn't have penetrated farther than the trachea and principal air passages. There was no struggle. Also, if a living body is drowned, the blood in the lungs and heart becomes diluted." He looked across to Dr. Crofton. "I know I'm speaking in the presence of an expert, so I'd better not leap with quite the aplomb of Stephanie Lawless. Correct me if I'm wrong, Doctor, but what I've said applies to fresh water—in this case, marsh water—doesn't it? The body reacts differently when salt is present."

Sandy Crofton, whose sympathy was solidly on the side of a fellow writer, confirmed it briefly. "Salt water causes a partial osmotic interchange of electrolytes in the lung bed. Your average reader isn't likely to know that."

Maybridge thanked him and then turned back to Bonny. "The pathologist who performed the autopsy should have known it. He was a little lax, shall we say?"

"And by implication, so was I?" Bonny's poise was slipping. Sir Godfrey had turned in his chair and was looking at her, his amusement barely concealed.

"We're all lax sometimes," Maybridge soothed. "The professional detective can't afford to make mistakes, but of course he does. Fictional sleuths can break every rule in the book; it doesn't matter. Long may your feline detective—your Stephanie Lawless—leap around and give us a lot of fun." He was aware belatedly that he had said the wrong thing. To criticize professional errors was acceptable; to make fun of a beloved alter ego was not.

"I'm glad you found her so hilarious." There was frost in Bonny's voice. She bent over and picked up Ulysses again. He had left a dribble of spit on Scott's pullover. Scott wiped it away without rancor.

"Well," Maybridge said after a few more examples, "that's about it, I think. May I congratulate all of you on your expertise." At least you got published, though God knows why in some cases, he thought. They had been a captive audience, like a rare species behind bars in a zoo. He had taunted them a little and fed them a few nuts. He had enjoyed himself, probably more than they had. He reminded them of the notes on ballistics that were on the table next to the projector. "You might find them useful."

Sir Godfrey left his chair and walked onto the stage. His handshake as he gripped Maybridge's hand was enthusiastic. "Our unreserved thanks, chief inspector. I think I can speak for all of us when I say we appreciated your lecture enormously." There was polite assent from the audience and a little hand clapping.

Ulysses put his thumb in his mouth and opened sapphire-blue eyes. "Clap hands, Daddy comes," Bonny mouthed bitterly into Ulysses' soft sandy hair, "with his pocket full of plums."

During the last few minutes of Maybridge's lecture, Sir Godfrey had planned a speech that would touch lightly on some of the points that the chief inspector had mentioned. This would be followed by a plug for his own book.

He began with a few opening comments. "The craft of the writer is an amalgam of the mercurial imagination with the solid discipline of getting words onto paper." He smiled blandly at the audience. "As all you writers know, plotting a crime novel involves hours of effort. Background research has to be done thoroughly, and it usually is. However, in some cases, as the chief inspector has pointed out, the research hasn't been quite as meticulous as—" He broke off abruptly as his eyes met those of his son. Ulysses, his thumb still in his mouth, was glaring at him from the safety of his mother's knee. Momentarily disconcerted, Sir Godfrey lost the drift of what he was saying. In the brief silence, Ulysses remembered that this was the man he had recently met and didn't like.

His roar began like the low rumbling of a hurricane in the distance, got gradually louder, and pitched into a high, piercing shriek. Scarlet faced, his mouth a distorted oval of loudly expressed hate, he sat yelling and thumping his fists on Bonny's perfect little breasts. Yell, she thought, go on, yell at the bastard. That's right, baby; give him hell. Your dad's face is getting as puce as yours. At any moment now, he's going to start yelling back. Outshout him, kiddo. Scream his bloody head off. Go on—scream, scream, scream!

The reaction of the audience was mixed. Lawrence Haydon thanked God for dogs; Marcus would occasionally howl, but not like this. Christopher Haydon ate peppermint and mused contentedly on a sexual aberration that couldn't reproduce. Kate looked at Lloyd with the first flicker of amusement she had shown in days. He winked at her awkwardly, the skin around his eye socket creasing deeply.

Maybridge, looking down at the audience and not picking out anyone in particular, thought it was like a classical concert being invaded by a miniature punk rocker, a one-infant band that was raucously raising the roof. He had a strong urge to laugh, but looking at Sir Godfrey's face, suppressed it.

And Ulysses, running out of breath, stopped for five seconds to refill his lungs.

Sir Godfrey broke the sweet sanity of silence. His voice was as rough as if he had been yelling, too. "Take that child out!"

Bonny's "Come and get him, Daddy" was drowned by Ulysses as he began roaring again.

Sir Godfrey, not hearing but motivated by anger equal to

his son's, left the stage and went down to confront Bonny, who smiled at him dangerously and then stood up to thrust Ulysses at him. If you hurt our child, she told him telepathically, I'll kill you. Ulysses was already hurting Grant, his flailing fists thumping at his eyelids. Grant tried to push him back at Bonny, but Ulysses, having made contact with his enemy, clung on. One of his socks fell off, and Scott Wilson caught it. "Go on, boxer," Scott said inaudibly. "You're doing fine." Grant felt something warm and wet trickling out of the side of Ulysses' diaper and soaking his shirt. It was the final indignity. He put his son over his shoulder and walked out. Bonny followed, still smiling dangerously.

Maybridge, alone on the stage, was aware that it was up to him to bring the meeting to an end.

"Well," he said jovially, "at least only one member of the audience was vociferous in his disapproval." He indicated his notes. "If you want to murder anyone by gun, these will tell you how. If you prefer some other method, then get hold of a book on forensic science and try to get it right. Don't let your murders be slipshod. Try to make them a fine art. Good luck to you and your corpses."

There was a rustle of applause like a cold wind through a blighted tree. Maybridge wondered if he should give an ironic little bow. He decided against it.

Chapter **THREE**

It was four o'clock and time for afternoon tea for those who wanted it. Fay, striving to be calm and practical, checked with the kitchen staff that there were sandwiches and buttered scones laid out on small metal trays in the canteen for the writers to come and collect. She also checked that preparations for the evening dinner were in hand. At home her dinner parties never exceeded a dozen guests—a neat number. Seminars were untidy. So many things could go wrong—and *were* going wrong. Godfrey, fuming, had driven home for a clean suit to wear that evening. He had refused to speak to her about the row he had had with Bonny outside the lecture room.

Bonny, like a thin little cat that had used its claws very effectively against a male adversary, was prowling around the kitchen, looking for cookies for Ulysses. "The plain sort he can dip in his milk," she told the cook, who took time from preparing the vegetables to find some.

"Is he teething?" the cook asked, having heard something of the rumpus.

"Among other things," Bonny said. She felt elated and looked at Fay without a twinge of guilt. In a fracas, the innocent tended to be trampled on, but Fay was well compensated. She was rich. Her home was a museum piece, impeccably in period. Antique furniture, wrested from less fortunate Sotheby bidders, gleamed triumphantly. There were no old sofas with sagging springs, no wet patches on walls, no moldy smell. The bloody great bath had gold taps, and the marital bed was of dark polished oak carved along the top in swags of bloody grapes. Ulysses had been conceived there one wet afternoon while Fay was on a shopping trip in Paris, buying a mink jacket or two. Bonny wiped some milk off Ulysses' blue knitted jersey. "Wonderful the stuff you can buy in secondhand stalls," she said quietly.

Fay, determined not to be drawn into Godfrey's battlefield, murmured something about things to see to and withdrew to the common room. "If anyone wants tea," she told the writers assembled there, "go along to the canteen."

Marcus, who knew the word tea, was the first to respond. He had been slumped down at Lawrence Haydon's feet, but at the mention of tea woke and thumped his tail. He was twelve years old and for the last four years, since the death of Haydon's wife, had been the major's sole companion.

"I've brought his dish," Haydon told Fay, "and tins of dog food." His voice, when addressing Fay, was far less aggressive than it had been when talking to Sir Godfrey earlier. They had always got on well together. During previous seminars, Marcus had either been taken to Christopher's flat over the pharmacy in London, or Christopher had gone down to his father's home in Weston to look after him. But this time there had been no one to leave him with.

Fay, in complete sympathy with the major, hadn't expected him to be at the seminar. If he won the Golden Guillotine, it could be awarded in abstentia. That he was here in person, together with his dog and his son, didn't imply a goodwill mission of forgiveness. He had made that clear in the lecture room. Godfrey lacked both tact and judgment, and she wondered if she should say anything in mitigation—or would it make matters worse?

"Lovely animal," she said at last, patting Marcus. It seemed safer to praise the dog.

"And quiet," Haydon replied. "There's a dog basket in the car, but I'd prefer him to sleep in my room, if that's all right with you? He's used to company at night."

Fay said she was agreeable and hoped that Godfrey would be wise enough not to make an issue of it. He had done enough damage already with a quite unjustified allegation. The old man wasn't a plagiarist.

"It's good of you to be so accommodating," Haydon said stiffly. This woman could beguile him and cool his anger and make him behave sanely and rationally. But it was necessary to sustain his anger. On military exercises in the past, he had learned to be motivated by it. The hatred then had been artificially nurtured. Now it sprang from the gut. He respected the integrity of his characters and created them with painstaking labor. They peopled his solitude. When he wasn't writing, he thought of his wife. She had been determinedly joyful in the alien lands where his military career had taken her but had longed for home. In her middle fifties, shortly after his retirement, she had died. He had loved her, and only his books made her absence bearable. Only rarely did he turn to his son. He remembered suddenly that Fay hadn't met Christopher and introduced them.

Christopher, who had been reading a newspaper in the window alcove, rose languidly from his chair to greet her. Fay noticed his movements, which seemed exaggeratedly camp. None of her own homosexual acquaintances proclaimed their homosexuality quite so blatantly. What was he trying to do, annoy his father by stressing the difference between them? But remembering his anger on his father's behalf less than an hour ago, she found it difficult to believe.

"I am aware," Christopher said in his high nasal tone, "that I am here without an invitation, and for that I apologize. But I felt I needed to be with my father—or rather that my father needed to be with me. You will forgive both Marcus and me, I hope, for the intrusion."

Fay, forcing a smile, told him he was welcome. "You'll stay for dinner, of course. The presentation follows it."

Christopher, who had expected equal hostility from Grant and his wife, was surprised. His voice was a little less edged with sarcasm when he spoke again. "It's good of you to ask me. Are you sure it's convenient for you? What about your numbers?"

"One more makes no difference," she assured him. Godfrey would be annoyed, but she didn't care.

"In that case, thank you," Christopher smiled at her with some warmth and a degree of puzzlement. Didn't this wife bat at her husband's wicket. How would she respond later if the play got nasty?

As it would.

He looked across her to his father. The major, avoiding his glance, said something about getting Marcus's dish and left the room. That the dog had been a closer companion to his father over the last few years than he had been was something Christopher had learned to accept without rancor, or guilt. The relationship between father and son was for long stretches of time uneasy, and then, in moments of stress, there was a sudden blazing up of affection. The old man had come up to London to tell him of Grant's accusation. Had he told him by letter, Christopher would have written a cool note in reply and advised him to ignore it. But seeing his father's misery, disproportionate perhaps to the cause, had made his own anger flare. It was the kind of insult, he told him, that couldn't be ignored. It had taken imagination and a degree of skill to devise a suitable retribution.

"Your father writes excellent books," Fay told him. "They may not be a commercial success, but they have lasting value. I'm sure you're very proud of him."

Christopher looked at her silently, analyzing her motives. If

she was trying to make peace, he didn't want it. He hadn't
done anything positive for his father for a long time.

Puzzled by his expression, Fay stopped trying. She felt
loaded down by problems not of her own making. Glancing
through the window, she saw that Chief Inspector Maybridge
was strolling in the garden with one of the other guest lecturers, who was also staying for the dinner and presentation.
Satisfied that her duties as a hostess weren't likely to be in
demand for a while, she left the room and went upstairs. She
would have liked to soak in a hot bath, but the bathrooms
were bleak and uncomfortable, and besides, there wasn't time.
Godfrey would be gone another hour, but there were better
ways of spending sixty minutes. She undressed, and removing
the tortoiseshell comb, brushed her long dark hair before
getting into bed. Dwight Connors, clad in a toweling robe,
arrived in ten minutes, his chores as Sir Godfrey's literary
agent far from his mind. He slipped in quietly and bolted the
door behind him.

"I don't know why," Fay told him, "but I think I want to
weep."

"Tension," Dwight said. "You need to do a Ulysses with
your emotions. I bet he's feeling fine right this minute."

"Do you suggest I scream, thump you, drum my heels?"

Dwight took off his robe. "No," he said, and began caress-
ing her gently, "there are other ways."

Across the corridor, Lloyd Cooper had also bolted the door,
but for a different reason. Whenever he removed his hood, he
liked to be sure that no one would burst in on him. Once,
when on holiday, a chambermaid had returned for some clean-
ing fluid and had seen him standing by the dressing table. He
had seen her eyes reflected in the mirror and had never forgotten the shock in them. "Indecent exposure," he had told
Kate bitterly, "of the worst kind." He had made sure it would
never happen again.

On the whole, he thought, he was weathering this seminar rather well. To stand up and speak to the inspector across the lecture room was an achievement. To dine with the others tonight would be another barrier crossed. The best achievement of the lot, of course, would be to win the Guillotine, but he didn't think that was likely. *Count Four, Then Fire!* was the first book he and Kate had produced after a couple of years of being unable to write at all. It wasn't up to the standard of the books they had written before, but it had been born after a period of stress that had temporarily killed their creativity.

He was tired. Contact with people other than Kate sapped him. Physically, he wasn't as robust as he used to be, though emotionally he was getting better. Just now he needed an hour or so on his own. The bed in this rather squalid little room was narrow and reminded him of a hospital bed. Hospitals, when the pain eased, weren't bad places to be. It was easier to be gregarious with your own kind than to try to find a niche again among the beautiful and unblemished.

But he *was* beginning to find a niche, forced into finding it by both Kate and his doctor. Last year they had chivied him into accepting the invitation to the seminar—the challenge, they had called it. The great step into the normal world. Get out among your own kind, they had said. Talk the sort of shop you know—books, agents, royalties, awards. And he had listened to them. And it hadn't been bad. Now, a year later, he was even enjoying parts of it, such as Maybridge's lecture this afternoon. So what was the matter with Kate?

Up to a couple of days ago she had talked of the seminar with her usual enthusiasm, and then she had become strangely silent about it. During their lovemaking, her fingers had explored his scars almost in a healing ritual. Disturbed, he had captured her fingers and held them. "The seminar—" she had said. "You don't have to go. You don't have to prove anything to yourself or anybody anymore."

Puzzled by Kate's reaction, he had told her testily that he was attending the seminar because he chose to attend it. In the past, he had needed to be pushed forward, but now some of the momentum was his. Her change of attitude and her continuing low spirits were surprising and hard to take. He was even beginning to resent them. Was she, perhaps, suffering from fatigue? Her nursing job at the health center was demanding. If she needed a holiday, they could take that cottage in Cumberland again. It was quiet—a pleasant retreat that suited him very well and a peaceful place in which to start drafting their new book. The garden wasn't overlooked. He could sit outdoors and feel the sun on his face and head. The removal of the hood, according to his doctor, was the next step forward on the road to normal living. But he refused to visualize it except in the well-screened garden of a country cottage.

He wished he had something of reasonable merit to read now. He had picked up a copy of Grant's new book, *The Helius Factor*, from the table in the common room before coming up. Grant tended to scatter his books around like cannabis seed, hoping, no doubt, for fulsome praise despite the noxious product. But to hell with literary aspirations. To hell even with literacy. Grant's new offering would be amusing, if nothing else. Kate had had a copy, but she'd lost it on a bus. He began reading.

Maybridge spent the hours between tea and dinner feeling bored. He had looked everywhere for Fay but had failed to find her. On the whole, he decided, he didn't like writers very much, and Fay, a nonwriter, was pleasantly normal. With the other lot you couldn't be sure what was going on in their minds. He had had a conversation with the grandmotherly one about prussic acid. Rasputin, she had told him, had been able to swallow it without dropping dead because he suffered from gastritis. Why, she asked, was that? Did the inspector think it was anything to do with the gastric juices minimizing the effect of the acid? Oh, undoubtedly, said Maybridge, and inquired politely about her knitting. It was a scarf, she had answered. For her husband. To hang him with? Maybridge wondered. It was long enough.

Sir Godfrey's intended lecture to the novices on the presentation of manuscripts was given in his absence by Dr. Crofton. Had Maybridge been aware of this, he might have gone along and listened. He had no interest in the subject, but he found the doctor's dual role intriguing.

Crofton, however, who was not a good lecturer, was relieved that Maybridge didn't appear. The chief inspector had either looked up forensic details about the books he had read, he thought, or he had a wider knowledge of the subject than might have been expected. Was he just concerned with the corpus delicti, or did he have a more generalized interest? He would, after all—as part of his job—know a fair amount about hard drugs. And about the unholy alliance between supplier and addict. Grant, the doctor guessed, hadn't yet had time to read through the novices' manuscripts, though he had received some by post during the last couple of weeks and might have scanned those. That he should read them at all was a large plus in his favor. "If you haven't typed your manuscripts," Dr. Crofton reminded his audience, "then the chances are Sir Godfrey won't be bothered with the handwritten efforts. I believe he made that plain to you during last year's seminar. This time he asked me to stress the fact that he wants a synopsis pinned to each manuscript. If anyone has forgotten the synopsis, I suggest you get it done between now and dinner. There's a typewriter in the office off the main hall."

Three novices—including Scott Wilson—admitted to having forgotten the synopsis. Scott at least had a portable machine in his bedroom. He said he'd do it there. His bedroom was number nineteen and on the same landing as Bonny's. He paused outside her door, resisted temptation, and went on.

Writing the synopsis wouldn't come easily to him. It was a chore he hadn't anticipated, and he found it difficult to concentrate. Down in the grounds he could hear the click of croquet mallets signaling more enjoyable pursuits. He left his typewriter and leaned on the windowsill. The green of the grass stood in strong relief to the early-evening sky, which was yellowing. The primary colors, like a primitive painting, gave the landscape an air of innocence. Bonny was playing croquet with the female half of the Chester Barrington team, so he hadn't denied himself anything by not knocking at her door. The other two players were Major Haydon and his son. There was no sign of the baby or the dog. Scott smiled, suddenly remembering Ulysses' performance.

He wondered if Sir Godfrey had returned yet and went down to his office to investigate. There was no one there. He went in and closed the door; it was a good opportunity to look through some of the manuscripts and ascertain the quality of the opposition. Eventually, he found the blue folder with his name on it, though the typewritten sheets stapled together inside it were not what he expected to see. They were disturbingly familiar, the result of serious and sustained research. Surprised and perturbed, he sat looking at them and wondered what to do.

Bonny would have preferred partnering Scott Wilson in croquet—or in a livelier activity—but tolerated Christopher Haydon with reasonable grace. He played badly, smashing the ball down the length of the course, never bothering to aim, while his father made small, meticulous moves, chipping gently at his opponents' ball with his own, moving it out of the way. Bonny couldn't help but sense the tension of the two men; their play, she thought, was uncharacteristic. The major should have been the one who made strong, careless strokes and his son the finicky ones. Kate played a game similar to the major's, and they were winning with ease.

Of all the writers present, Bonny felt the closest affinity with Kate. She was a tolerant and undemanding friend—there when needed. Like her, Kate and her husband were London based, and they met socially from time to time. When Bonny had become pregnant, she had gone to Kate for advice —to abort or not to abort? The older woman, who would have loved a child, was definite in her view that Bonny should keep it and had been the first to visit her in hospital after Ulysses was born. She, too, was the one who had insisted that Bonny should give him a second name. "Or he'll loathe you forever."

"Such as God?" Bonny had asked.

"Such as Adam. The first man—your first infant. Start leaving Godfrey out of the picture if you want to love your child."

Wise Kate. And at the moment, a very quiet and moody Kate.

"Pity Lloyd couldn't join us," Bonny said for the sake of saying something; Kate's quite obvious depression was getting her down. Kate said he was resting. She clipped Bonny's ball out of the way and put hers through the hoop.

"That's it," said the major. "Well done."

"Excellent," said Christopher, relieved that the game was over. He had nothing in common with these two women writers, and the young one he found particularly irritating. He hoped he wouldn't be seated near her at dinner. It was convenient that Fay had invited him for the meal, but he would have preferred to have had something on his own in the local pub. There his clothes would have been more appropriate. He was wearing tight blue jeans and a yellow sweater and had no means of changing. This was a day trip. He intended driving back to London tonight. "Just how formal is the dinner?" he asked the others.

Bonny replied caustically that white tie and tails weren't in order and that medals wouldn't be worn. She smiled at the

major, and he gazed somberly back at her. He was grateful
for Christopher's presence and touched by his loyalty; how
his son looked didn't matter, but he wished to Christ he'd
use a less flowery after-shave. As he stumped off toward the
game shed, carrying his own mallet and Kate's, the major had
a queasy prebattle feeling in his stomach that only a whiskey
could ease.

Just before dinner, Maybridge put a long-distance call
through to Meg. She was in Pittsburgh, enjoying her tour. She
asked him how his lecture had gone. All right, he replied; it
had been amusing while it lasted. He tried to sound more
enthusiastic than he felt, but he missed her and told her so.

Kate waited until the inspector had replaced the receiver,
then went over to speak to him. She had changed into a dress
of navy silk that made her pale skin seem even paler.
Anxiety, though obvious in her eyes, was carefully leveled
out of her voice. She reminded Maybridge that she was Kate
Cooper, pseudonym Chester Barrington, and had he by any
chance seen her husband, Lloyd? He had left a note in the
bedroom saying he had gone out for cigarettes, but he had
been gone rather a long time. Maybridge, aware that she was
a great deal more worried than she sounded, wondered why.
He told her he hadn't seen him and asked if he wasn't well.
"He has recovered from extensive burns," Kate replied rather
too crisply. "As far as it's possible to recover. Apart from
that, he's perfectly well. He's probably holed up somewhere
in this awful mausoleum of a building, talking royalties."

"A pleasant way of passing the time," Maybridge suggested.

"It might have been once," Kate said, "but not these days.
Whereas other people's royalties take them to the Bahamas,
ours keep Lloyd in cigarettes. Just." She moved away. "If you
happen to see him, don't mention I've been looking for him.
He can't stand fuss."

"No," Maybridge said, "I understand." And he did and was troubled. In police work you were routinely exposed to the peccadilloes of the human race and were rarely shocked. But if Sir Godfrey's description in his latest book had been deliberately based on Lloyd's disfigurement, it was astonishingly cruel. He looked after Kate as she walked down the corridor and wondered if she knew. More importantly, did her husband know?

By dinnertime Lloyd hadn't returned, though in the large refectory his absence wasn't apparent to anyone who wasn't looking for him. It was Grant's policy that there should be no head table, no form of literary elitism. Fay dutifully sat next to her husband on her left and put Maybridge on her right. It would give her a chance to get to know him. To the right of Maybridge was Christopher Haydon, and next to him, the major. Fay knew that it would have been more tactful to have placed the Haydons at one of the other tables, as far away as possible from Godfrey, but she was tired of being diplomatic. And at least they weren't facing each other. She looked across the room making eye contact with Dwight. He smiled at her rather ruefully, wanting to be near her but aware that the separation was wise.

Trevor Martin, the arts master who had written *Death Is Discreet*, arrived late in the refectory after having gone down to the chemist for a sedative. He had promised Kate that he would have a general scout around for Lloyd but in fact hadn't bothered to look. A tension headache was building up behind his eyes, and he felt clammy and uninvolved. The enforced sociability of the meal would be difficult to cope with, as would the meal itself. He had to be careful what he ate. "He probably can't face the awful conviviality of the meal," he had told Kate with some feeling. "It's the easiest part of the shindig to miss."

Martin had known Kate and her husband since the inception of the Golden Guillotine Club. He had had sympathy for

Lloyd in the early days but not so much now. Lloyd leaned
too much on his wife. If she weren't so tough, he would have
crippled her. Women, Martin still believed, should be pro-
tected from the harsher elements; a man should be able to
cope with anything unpleasant and do what needed to be done
without reference to his companion. All Martin's compassion
was for the woman in his life. But in the Coopers' case, all
Lloyd's compassion was most definitely for Lloyd. And Kate
herself knew this all too well. Her anxiety now was tinged
with anger, and it was anger that made it possible to go down
to the dining room and not stay brooding in the bedroom.

Kate took the place next to Bonny and put her handbag
on the adjacent chair so that no one would sit there.

"Men are thoughtless bastards," Bonny told her, sensing
the reason for Kate's disquiet. She liked Lloyd but at this
moment could cheerfully have kicked him.

"His watch is erratic," Kate pointed out.

"But so is Lloyd," Bonny persisted. "You don't have to
excuse him to me."

Kate, abruptly changing the subject, asked her coldly
where Ulysses was.

"In bed. I meant to grab a chair next to Godfrey and plonk
Ulysses on his knee together with a spoon and a tin of baby
food, but he told me he'd had enough of his dad and could he
go to sleep, please?" She looked at the prawns in savory jelly
that had just been served. The dish looked innocuous enough.
Later on, when he woke up, Ulysses might like some. She
asked if she might have Lloyd's if he didn't come, and Kate,
too flattened by worry to point out that exotic food and infants
didn't get on well together, passed the prawns over without
a word. Obviously, Lloyd wouldn't be in time for the first
course; that he wouldn't be in time for any course became
apparent as time went on.

Sir Godfrey, unaware that Lloyd wasn't there, was, however, extremely relieved by the absence of Ulysses. He had no

trace of affection for the child. When he had carried him out of the lecture room earlier that day, the flesh of his flesh had stirred nothing in him other than a strong desire to be rid of infant and mother both. He was aware that Bonny wanted more than money from him. She wanted paternal commitment, too, an ongoing interest in the brat. "You can't buy me off," she had told him above Ulysses' screams out in the hall. "You've made him. He's yours."

"My only responsibility is to my twin daughters," he had shouted back.

"Sod your bloody daughters," Bonny had yelled, shocking one of the kitchen helpers who happened to be passing. The altercation had ended there. But it would, he was quite sure, be resumed.

Seated for dinner, he was careful now not to catch Bonny's eye. She was dressed in a bright red, very full cotton dress that disguised her thinness. Her body, he remembered, for all its lack of curves, was irresistibly sexy. Fay, large and voluptuous, only occasionally aroused him. He tended to go off his women after a year or so. His first marriage had been brief, though fecund. Gina and the twins were now living in Bath —very comfortably, thanks to his shrewd investments and her even sharper lawyer. Gina, unglamorous, worthy, and with a strong maternal instinct equal to Bonny's, hadn't been easy to ditch. She had demanded the best of everything for the twins. And his conscience had kicked him into giving *her* the best of everything, too. We are betrayed by our appetites, he thought bitterly.

In an attempt to force himself out of a self-inflicted moroseness, he turned to the young novice writer sitting on his left. Sir Godfrey had talked to Scott Wilson only once before, when he had unexpectedly found him in his office that afternoon. The young man had had no business to skulk around uninvited, but his apologetic explanation about the synopsis had mollified him, and they had subsequently spent an enjoyable ten minutes discussing Grant's latest foray into bestsellerdom. He passed Scott the wine and resumed the conversation where it had been left off.

"I just wish I could make your sort of money by terrifying a large section of the reading public," Scott was saying. "Tell me—how do I produce a best seller? What do I have to do? How did you start?"

"Later on, when I've had a chance to look at your manuscript, I'll be able to assess your ability. If you're worth encouraging, I'll encourage you."

Scott thanked him politely. The breast of lamb milanaise had arrived. "*Bon appétit*," he said.

Meanwhile, the conversation Maybridge was engaged in with the younger Haydon was developing rather less felicitously. Christopher confessed that his lecture had made him sick, "almost literally."

"I'm sorry," Maybridge said, "but I did warn you at the start that some of the slides weren't pleasant. What sort of books do you write?"

"None, dear," Christopher replied. He tended to parody himself whenever he felt nervous or excited, and tonight he was both. The thickset policeman on his left represented a challenge. Maybridge had spent a long time in conversation with Fay but turned to Christopher from time to time out of an obvious sense of duty. Christopher disliked boring people. "If I were to write a book," he said, "my victim would be poisoned." He explained that he managed a pharmacy. "As a registered pharmacist, I can sell part-one and part-two poisons. And if Mr. Haigh had come to me, I could have told him in minute detail how to dispose of the false teeth."

"Then you'd have been an accessory to the crime," Maybridge observed blandly.

"Only in theory," Christopher replied. "Of course, I keep strictly on the right side of the law." He giggled. "And at this moment, literally so." He leaned forward and adjusted a piece of fern that formed part of the table decoration together with small bronze chrysanthemums.

Maybridge turned back to Fay, who, with encouragement from him, had been telling him about her childhood in India. Her rather shy response to his genuine interest was both heartwarming and amusing. Her first impressions of Scotland, she told him, had been formed in midwinter, when she was twelve years old. She had flown over from Delhi to be bridesmaid to a cousin she had never met. "My mother's sister's daughter. I don't know what the family expected me to look like—small and dark skinned probably. I was made to wear a dress of pink satin and looked big, clumsy, and horrible. It snowed." Maybridge, visualizing the scene, felt sympathy for the gauche child she had been and a growing liking for the shy woman she had become.

But over dessert Christopher demanded his attention again. "One of the hazards of running a pharmacy is having the place broken into. I had a large quantity of Diconal stolen some while ago. Your colleagues, in that particular instance, weren't very effective; it's never been recovered."

Maybridge commiserated dutifully. He didn't like talking shop any more than Dr. Crofton, but before he had a chance to change the subject, Christopher went on. "One of the officers in the drug squad told me that drug addiction had risen in the last three or four years by forty percent. Most of the drugs are mind benders. There are times when I wonder if our illustrious host is on drugs. You understand, I suppose, that he accused my father of plagiarism?"

Maybridge, conscious that Grant was sitting within hearing range, cast around for something to say that would silence Christopher. But he pressed on inexorably. "Transference as a theme goes back to classical times, as my father made plain in the lecture room. Grant didn't invent it any more than my father did." About to elaborate, he suddenly became aware of Maybridge's embarrassment and lapsed into sullen silence.

After dinner was over, Grant led the way to the lecture hall. Dwight Connors had already arranged seven chairs on the stage for the seven contenders for the award. At its center stood the green baize table that Maybridge had earlier used for his projector. On it, next to a pile of unopened envelopes, was the Golden Guillotine.

Maybridge looked at it curiously. The gold blade, he guessed, was the most valuable part of it. The rest of the structure would be of baser metal. It stood all of six inches high. If it were solid gold, it would be worth thousands, not the few hundred Connors had mentioned. No instrument of death was pretty, and this one had no aesthetic pretensions. A nasty-looking object. As he took his seat next to Fay in the front row, he saw with annoyance that Christopher Haydon was making for the chair on his left. He couldn't do anything to prevent him. Christopher leaned across and spoke to Fay. "It was an excellent meal."

She realized it was an apology and accepted it. "Yes, the kitchen staff did well."

"Under your leadership."

"Hardly leadership—just a little persuasion."

Christopher sat back in his chair, sweating slightly. He had been up to his father's room and had returned with a small cardboard box that he held on his knee. He didn't attempt to speak to the inspector again, and Maybridge, to fill an awkward pause, asked Fay if she helped her husband with the secretarial side of his writing.

"Not much these days. I used to do it all, but now Dwight Connors organizes that side of things. I did a little work on Godfrey's last book, but I haven't read it through. Is that an awful admission?"

"No." On the contrary, it was reassuring. Maybridge was

looking at the empty chair on the stage next to Kate's. Lloyd hadn't returned. "You don't advise your husband on his work —suggest deletions, for instance?"

Fay looked at him in surprise. "Good heavens no! I just help generally—I'm not the critic."

Maybridge, happy in her company, was pleased he didn't need to revise his opinion of her. He liked people who were basically kind and honest. These were Meg's greatest qualities, too.

Bonny came late to the stage after checking that Ulysses was all right. She had paid one of the kitchen staff to baby-sit for a couple of hours. Ulysses, once in bed, usually slept around the clock, but if he didn't, someone had to be within earshot. "There's warm milk in the thermos," she had told the girl, "and there's prawns in aspic—or something. Try him with both if he wakes, and if that doesn't work, call me."

She took her place next to Kate, and after a swift glance in her direction, told her to stop worrying. "Lloyd's not as emotionally tough as the rest of us. He's had a bellyful and called it a day. That's all. He'll come back when he's ready." But Kate, usually so polite, didn't bother to answer—had hardly heard. She was plucking at a loose thread on her sleeve, unaware that she was unraveling it. The words "psychologically a walking disaster" kept stinging her brain like wasps. She looked over at Sir Godfrey, silver haired and very good looking, his skin smooth and unblemished. She had returned to the bedroom a few minutes ago in the hope that Lloyd had returned. But instead she had found *The Helius Factor* where it had fallen at the far side of the bed. Her immediate reaction was to tell Maybridge and ask for a police search. But common sense had grudgingly prevailed. Lloyd needed time. If he hadn't returned by the end of the evening, she would tell the chief inspector then. Not before. In the meantime, the raw ache of anxiety was worse than physical pain.

"I don't know why we're expected to sit up here," Bonny

grumbled. "It would be far more civilized if we all sat in the
hall and only the winner came up. It makes the rest of us look
like fools." Then Bonny noticed Kate's obsessional tugging of
the thread and put out her hand with unusual gentleness to
stop her. "I hope you win," she said quietly, and meant it.
She needed the cash that the award represented, perhaps more
than Kate and Lloyd did, but they needed the boost to morale.
Her own morale was fighting fit. She wondered how many
Golden Guillotines still existed in their original state. The
value of gold had been rising steadily; it was a good seller's
market.

Most of the other contenders were thinking the same,
though Major Haydon coveted nothing beyond the respect of
his fellow writers. He had waited long enough for it. Christopher looked at him and smiled. His father, however, almost
sick with tension, was incapable of smiling back.

Dwight counted the votes in full view of everyone while
Grant stood silently just behind him. It didn't take Dwight
long. The Chester Barrington book *Count Four, Then Fire!*
was runner-up to Lawrence Haydon's *Transfer to Death.*
Knowing that Grant wouldn't like the result, though obviously he must have anticipated it, Dwight scribbled the
numbers on a piece of paper and handed it over. But Sir
Godfrey, with two speeches of congratulation prepared, didn't
let his annoyance at the verdict show. He moved importantly
over to the center of the stage and stood behind the table.

"I was once asked a very difficult question," he said
smoothly, "a question that no doubt many of you have been
asked. Just how does a writer spin his web of fiction? What
sort of peculiar chemistry in the mind produces people and
places that are more real to the writer as he sits at his typewriter than the actual room he physically occupies? I couldn't
answer the question. I just don't know. Writers absorb ex-
periences. We remember traces of the past. Perhaps nothing
is new. The alchemy of the imagination gilds mundane hap-

penings. We describe someone, believing that description to be pure fiction, and then remember, perhaps with dismay, that we have modeled from life." He glanced briefly at Lloyd's empty chair and carefully avoided catching Kate's eye. "To quote Ruskin, 'All immortal writers speak out of their hearts.' We who are here this evening are run-of-the-mill writers with no claim on immortality. I don't know where we speak from. The stories come from somewhere inside us, triggered by external events. Occasionally, however, we do know the source of our fiction. We wear borrowed plumes. It is rare for a keen and inventive mind to have to resort to this, but sadly it happens. That it can also happen through a trick of the subconscious, I am prepared to believe. How many of us relate our murderers to Cain?"

Christopher Haydon, restless with contained fury, muttered almost audibly, "Megalomaniac—paranoid—twisted!" He raised his voice a little so that Maybridge could hear him. "He's mad, my dear, mad."

Maybridge sat rigidly facing the front and ignored him.

Grant went on. "You have all produced very interesting books, using your own special talents in your own special ways. The fact that only one of you has won the award doesn't detract in any way from the quality of the other contenders. He smiled bleakly and tried to show an enthusiasm he didn't feel. "And now for the winner. By a very narrow margin you have voted Lawrence Haydon's *Transfer to Death* into first place. *Count Four, Then Fire!* by Chester Barrington is a very gallant runner-up—just three votes behind. My congratulations, Lawrence Haydon." He clapped politely and gestured for the winner to come forward.

The major waited for the applause in the hall to die away. He was rarely aware of his age, but tonight he felt old. Anger, the driving force of the last few weeks, no longer sustained him. He could feel no emotion of any kind other than an uneasy sickness. He leaned his knuckles on the tabletop while

Grant picked up the Golden Guillotine and offered it to him. He didn't touch it, and Grant, shrugging, put it down again.

"I'm not an orator," Haydon said at last, his voice rough. "I can't makes speeches. Neither can I wear what Sir Godfrey calls borrowed plumes. My books are my own. *Transfer to Death* is entirely and absolutely mine. It owes nothing to any other work of fiction. You people, sitting down there, know this; otherwise you would have been influenced by Sir Godfrey's scurrilous letter in our club bulletin. Thank you for believing in me." He picked up the Guillotine, the gold blade glowing in the artificial light. "As for this, I'm accepting it on behalf of all the other contestants who are sitting up here on the stage. I shall sell it for the best price I can get and give the others the proceeds. I shall keep none of it for myself. After tonight I shall no longer be a member of this writers' society. Writing is, after all, a solitary occupation, and I'm happy on my own." He noticed that Christopher had risen from his chair and was coming forward to the stage with the box. He waved him away irritably. "No," he said, "no." He felt a wave of nausea and thought for an awful moment that he was going to be sick. He stood clutching the award, unable to speak, in a state of panic. He had to get out, but the stage was misty; he wasn't sure where the exit was and almost knocked over one of the chairs trying to find it. Dwight Connors, his face expressionless, went over to help him, but Haydon, with an impatient gesture, pushed him away.

Sir Godfrey, pale and angry, had encountered a situation he didn't know how to handle and stood stiffly by the table, unable to take command. Someone in the audience began to clap. It was cautious, like a single shot from behind enemy lines. Others followed suit, but the gesture was desultory. Grant, aware that some troops were still on his side, regained some of his self-confidence. He shrugged and smiled. Let the plagiarizing old fool have the last word, he implied. Let *us*, ladies and gentlemen, be civilized. He led the way off the stage.

Lawrence Haydon had to pass Maybridge and Fay in order to reach his son. He looked at neither of them, but Fay stood up and put a restraining hand on his arm. Her cheeks were flushed with distress, but her voice was very gentle. She asked him if he was all right.

It took him a moment or two to recognize her. "Perfectly, Fay. And I apologize to you."

She touched his hand. It was very cold. "The apologies should be in the other direction. I mean Godfrey should apologize to you. No one for a minute took that stupid letter of his seriously."

He smiled at her with some sadness. "He did."

That was so obviously true that she didn't know what to say. She started to ask him if he was coming through to the bar to celebrate with the rest of them and then checked herself rapidly. "But you'll stay the night, won't you? You're not going to walk away from us tonight—please!"

He told her that he had planned to stay overnight and saw no reason to alter his plans. He was too tired to drive anywhere far, and he and Christopher had arrived in separate cars. He turned to his son. "If you don't mind delaying your departure by a couple of hours, we'll go and have a drink somewhere else."

"Surely. I'll stay as long as you need me." It was spoken with deep compassion.

How had the major's genes produced Christopher? Maybridge wondered as he watched them go. They were a study in contrasts as they walked out of the hall together. It was perhaps maudlin to talk of the bond of love, but it was there nevertheless. The younger man's anger was apparent in his every gesture, and the older man, the fury drained out of him, leaned hevily on his son's arm. In his free hand, the Guillotine, small and obscene, flashed and twinkled, an emblem of bloody execution.

Chapter FOUR

In the bar, Grant was in full voice again. Traditionally, this was the time of celebration, and he was damned if Lawrence Haydon would cast a blight on it. He had brought in several crates of champagne, and the drinks, he told everyone, were on the house. "Help yourself and enjoy!"

Hushed voices and dolorous expressions gradually changed. Conversations reached a high decibel level. There was laughter. Sympathy was almost entirely on Haydon's side, but Sir Godfrey's drinks were of high quality, and potent. So neatly divide your loyalties and drink, fellow writers, drink!

Dwight Connors, as barman for the evening, made sure to replenish Maybridge's glass frequently and liberally. "Come on, chief inspector; you're not on duty. Would you believe me if I told you that all the previous seminars were at least bearable?"

"You mean, because I didn't lecture at them."

Dwight grinned. "Your lecture was the best part. No, I meant the animosity—Haydon and Grant."

"Did Grant have cause for complaint?"

"He thought he had. His letter was a disastrous error. I told him so, but he wouldn't listen."

Maybridge sipped his whiskey. Dwight Connors obviously

didn't believe in blind loyalty. Sensible of him. "You told me when I arrived that you didn't write. How come you never caught the urge?"

"Urges, fortunately, aren't infections," Dwight pointed out. "Imagine an epidemic of torrid prose. I did try my hand at it once—a book on birds inspired by some pictures I took of storks nesting on chimney pots in Izmir. Photographs of a different kind of Turkish bird might have been more successful; ornithology is tame stuff. I didn't write anything after that. It was a long time ago." He moved away to serve more drinks.

Cora Larsbury had overheard. "A long time ago." She sighed. "What sad words. Someone asked me the other day what I had done with my life." She stared moodily at her champagne.

"And what did you say?" Maybridge asked politely.

"I said, 'Nothing courageous—nothing positive. I drifted along on a narrow little stream between flat green fields of boredom.'"

God spare me from writers, Maybridge thought, particularly when they're septuagenarians made maudlin on wine. He smiled at her and forced himself to continue the conversation. "Oh, come, surely it hasn't been that bad?"

"No, it hasn't been bad," she retorted. "Neither has it been good. I don't believe in life after death, but I do believe in life before death. However, for me it just didn't happen."

"I'm sorry." Maybridge tried to sound sympathetic. "You have no family? I understood you had a husband?"

"Oh, yes, inspector. He's a retired banker. His passion is stocks and shares. He consumes the *Financial Times* with his breakfast egg—almost literally."

"Have you any children?"

Cora finished her champagne and put the glass down on a nearby table. "Once upon a time I had children. I bathed

them, wiped their noses, read to them. They grew. They departed. My son was forty last June. My daughter is thirty-
eight."

"Do they enjoy your books?"

"My dear inspector," Cora said with deep bitterness, "my
books are not yet published. If they were, my family would
probably disown me." She smiled faintly. "And that, believe
me, could be a relief."

Maybridge had done his best and looked around for escape.
But Cora, understandably, didn't want to let him go. She
was lonely. She needed a listener. She had come to the seminar
filled with hope, like a child going to a fair, only to find
the merry-go-round run down and the colors tatty. Lawrence
Haydon, plagiarist or not, had been denied his triumph. His
own fault, probably; he needn't have acted that way. And
Sir Godfrey could have handled the situation better, though
she didn't know how. The atmosphere of the seminar, despite
the shrill jollification, was as hostile as a Dickensian fog. She
asked the inspector if he had caught any murderers recently.

It was a sad little joke requiring no answer. He smiled
politely at her.

"My son," she said, "is a queen's counsel. Family tradition
on my side. My father was a judge. He had people hanged.
My daughter is a social worker. They both deal in dregs—
differently."

Maybridge, not liking the word "dregs," was nevertheless
wise enough not to quarrel with it.

"Finance, law, social security," Cora went on. "Those are
the topics of conversation in my home on occasions such as
Christmas, when we're a family. We're a very dull family,
inspector. Do you know I'm not even allowed to read Grimm
to my grandchildren in case it frightens them."

"What about Milne?" Maybridge asked for the sake of
saying something.

"Perfectly acceptable," Cora replied with disgust. "A bear

called Pooh who flies kites and eats honey. That's about the
literary level of my family. Do you wonder I escape to my
typewriter?"

Some minutes later, Maybridge made his own escape by
mumbling something about having to see Fay. He joined her
at the far end of the bar. She had been watching him for the
last few minutes and was amused. He had the look of a parson
who had just been released from the clutches of an importunate church member. She told him so, though the analogy
wasn't apt. "Odd woman," he said reflectively.

"Not more so than any of the rest of us," Fay said. "Cora
has her high moods and her low ones. A nice old thing, really.
A fantastic cook. Makes lovely sweets."

At regular intervals during the evening, Kate went upstairs to see if Lloyd had returned. She had given herself a
deadline of eleven o'clock. If he hadn't come back by then,
she would tell Maybridge and ask his advice. He would probably tell her that her anxiety was unreasonable, that a grown
man was entitled to stay out all night without explanation
if he so wished. Maybridge was a very reasonable man. In
fact, everyone she had spoken to during the evening had been
very reasonable.

"Don't worry, Kate."

"He's bound to be fine, Kate."

"Let me top up your gin, Kate."

"Have fun, Kate."

At five to eleven she escaped from the din and went out
into the corridor and up the stairs. The passages were dimly
lit for economy. Someone, though not Lloyd, was walking to
the bathroom. She heard a door close, then the sound of
running water. She had left the light on in Lloyd's bedroom
because it was easier to walk into a lighted room, but he still
hadn't returned. Anger, fear, and loneliness churned in a
potent cocktail of pain as she walked aimlessly around the
room, touching the bed cover, his brushes on the dressing

table, his neatly strapped suitcase. Someone in a bedroom down the corridor turned on a transistor in a sudden whoop of sound and then lowered the volume to a syncopated mutter. She went over to the basin by the window to wash her hands and then gently pushed down the cuticles. This was a phobic ritual in times of stress—one she was hardly aware of.

She began rehearsing in her mind what she would say to Maybridge. "Inspector, you'll probably think this is incredibly foolish of me, but I'm so concerned for my husband . . ."

"Inspector, I'm sorry to bother you, but . . ."

"I know this must sound neurotic, inspector, and believe me I'm normally calm . . ."

"I'm frightened for him, inspector . . ."

"I'm bloody terrified, inspector . . . I'm . . ."

She began to shake. Maybridge would be with a group of people. When she had seen him last, he had been talking with two of the lecturers. She would have to prize him away from a group of noisy revelers. She would have to indicate her anxiety before she expressed it. Why did she find it so difficult to do something so comparatively simple when other, more major matters could be performed with cold competence?

Just go down, she told herself finally, and tell him. You've nothing to lose.

She washed her hands once more before leaving the room. Everywhere was very quiet now. And as she approached the bar, she realized that it was quiet there, too.

Lloyd had just walked in.

Relief flooded over her like bright sunshine. He stood in the center of the room, swaying slightly, his smile vacuous. Kate was used to seeing him with his head uncovered and was unaware of anything other than that he was there. "My apologies," he said, "for being late." He noticed his wife standing by the door. "Who won the award? Did we?"

She was beginning to understand the silence. She went over to him and took his arm. "No."

He removed her hand petulantly. "Don't touch me. I can stand."

Grant broke the silence, speaking with forced bonhomie. "Another hair of the dog, old chap." He walked over to the bar. "What will it be?"

Lloyd looked him up and down with grave approval. "Nice hair," he said, "very nice indeed. What pool do you look into, Narcissus? Your bathroom bog?"

Grant flinched visibly.

Lloyd's smile widened. "The literary eye," he began, "the lit-er-ary eye . . . Apply it, friend." He moved nearer Grant so that he was standing under the central light. "You have my permission to touch each scar, each fold, each wrinkle. Give me your hand."

Grant moved back.

"Oh, come," Lloyd chided, "you've seen a bald head before, but never one like mine. Don't pass up your chance, scribe. Get it down on paper fast. Come on. Touch, touch, touch . . ."

As Grant moved again, Lloyd lurched after him and made a grab for his arm. He missed and fell against a small table, which overturned and sent several wineglasses crashing.

Grant grimaced at Kate. "Get him out. He's not himself. Just get him up to bed." He could feel a trickle of sweat crawling coldly down his backbone, and there was a strong bitter taste at the back of his throat. Behind him, the bar stool was pressed up against his thighs. His knees felt weak. He needed to sit but didn't dare. An emotion compounded of anger and disgust made his heart lurch in strong, unsteady beats.

"Oh, but I am myself," Lloyd contradicted him gently. "Ab-so-lutely myself. A Quasimodo, a walking disaster, and I can't remember the rest of it, scribe, because my mind is smashed with booze, scribe." He rolled his head in an effort to look at everyone in the room. "You all knew, friends. Chapter and verse, friends. But you didn't tell me, did you. Damn your bloody eyes!" He looked at Kate, who stood rigid and pale.

"You let me damn well come!"

"I'm sorry." Her reply was a barely audible whisper.

Maybridge was the first to make a move and diffuse the menacing atmosphere. "Come," he said encouragingly, "let's get you upstairs." Together Maybridge and Connors walked him across the room and into the hall. They guided him toward the stairs, and he felt for each step like a climber on a rock face, planting his feet experimentally and then allowing himself to be heaved up to the next. Dr. Crofton, who had missed the confrontation, came along the corridor. He assessed the situation and offered to help. In his professional life he had seen much worse disfigurement but fewer minds so emotionally blown. Maybridge and Connors declined his assistance. They were managing.

It had been some time since Maybridge had undressed a drunk, but Connors seemed adept enough. Thankfully, Lloyd's grotesque scarring was less evident in the softer bedroom light. Maybridge, careful not to let his compassion show, folded the clothes and moved to put them on the chair by the door. He noticed that Kate was standing outside on the landing. Leaving Connors to get Lloyd into bed, he went out and joined her.

"This has happened before?"

"Never this badly."

Dwight joined them, closing the door behind him. "He won't need the coffee. He's asleep." He put his hand comfortingly on Kate's shoulder and pressed it gently.

She thanked them both.

"Well," said Maybridge, "if there's anything else I can do . . . ?"

"You've been very kind."

Maybridge hesitated, then said it. "It was a perfectly natural reaction, under the circumstances, for your husband to drink too much."

She realized he had read the book. Her own reaction, when she had read it for the first time, had been a kind of anger she had never known before. She had wanted to build barricades between Lloyd and the world. And then she had wanted to kick the world apart.

"I'm not blaming him," she told Maybridge. "I couldn't stop him attending the seminar without giving the reason. I was hoping he wouldn't find out."

"As I remember it, Grant made a kind of apology to you on the stage."

"That's not good enough, inspector." Her voice was cold steel.

He didn't know how to answer, particularly as he agreed with her. He shrugged. "Well, good night."

"Good night." She went into Lloyd's bedroom and closed the door. Her own name tag, Maybridge noticed, was on the door of the bedroom opposite. He decided to go along to his room and told Dwight he wouldn't be waiting for the party to end.

"I fancy it already has," Dwight said.

At one-fifteen, Scott Wilson went into Bonny's bedroom. He believed in the direct approach. "I can't resist the irresistible," he said, shaking her gently. "Move over." She had just dozed off after persuading an unusually restless Ulysses to do likewise.

"Get out!" she whispered crossly, leaning up on one elbow.

"I can't sleep."

"What's that to me?"

"An hour of bliss?"

He had brought his torch and was carefully shining it

around the room so that the light didn't awaken the baby. "The only sane person here is your child," he said.

"Glad you acknowledge your insanity." Bonny lay down again, feeling pleased despite herself that he liked Ulysses.

"What possessed you to bring him?"

"He needs to know his dad."

"If he's to retain his sanity, he's better off not knowing him."

"His dad needs to know him."

"His dad doesn't agree."

"He will," Bonny said.

"I doubt it."

Scott sat on the side of her bed. For a girl who looked as if she never ate very much, what she did eat had given her nice breasts, like firm little peaches. He told her so, stroking them.

"Go away." But the command was less emphatic.

It took him a half hour to persuade her, which was about par for both of them.

"The bed's too narrow," she said.

"It will do," he answered. And that was that.

At ten past four, an undigested savory prawn began playing merry hell with Ulysses' gut. Astonished and outraged, he awoke in the strange bedroom in the awful building filled with uncongenial people and began berating his mother for subjecting him to further horrors. Bonny, aware even in the depths of sleep that her son was voicing passionate censure, came quickly awake. It took a couple of seconds for her to realize that the large male figure shining a torch on Ulysses' cot wasn't intent on infanticide. Scott Wilson had made love superbly, but that was some while ago. Now, in the presence of her screaming son, he looked less than competent.

Bonny found the light switch. Ulysses screwed up his eyes against the light and screamed louder still. His mother, gazing at him in panic, saw real tears caused by real pain. His face was scarlet and screwed up in despair; he thumped his cot blanket with pink indignant fists and then pushed his fingers into his mouth.

"Oh, Jesus!" Bonny gasped as a stream of vomit spurted over his blue sleeping suit.

"An upset stomach," Scott diagnosed. He noticed the small entrée dish on the dressing table and remembered what it had once held. "There are books on the subject," he said, "if your common sense is lacking."

"What?" Bonny picked up Ulysses and wiped his mouth with the cot sheet.

"A bloody silly diet," Scott muttered quietly, sensing her antagonism.

Bonny took off the soiled sleeping suit and wrapped Ulysses in her red-striped sweatshirt. He looked like a bantam-weight boxer—bellicose but on the verge of defeat. She hugged him to her. "I love you, I love you, I *love* you."

"Let him breathe," Scott advised.

A little later, Bonny, Scott, and Ulysses went down to the kitchen where there was boiled water, bicarbonate of soda, and clean towels to tie around his neck. All the way to the kitchen, Ulysses pummeled his mother and screamed like the Furies.

Maybridge, together with several of the writers, awoke to the sound of departing wails. Doors were opened and closed, though Maybridge, warm and comfortable in bed, stayed there. He remembered that this was early Sunday morning; just how early he couldn't be bothered to find out. Soon the weekend would be over. He would drive home and do some work in the garden. A day of solitude would be very pleasant after this period of enforced and very stressful sociability. He hoped his son wouldn't arrive unexpectedly with one of his girlfriends. One day, he supposed, David would marry; there

would be grandchildren. A child like Ulysses would rent the
night with rage, and he would be fond of it. Maybridge turned
on his side and slept.

Down in the kitchen, Ulysses refused to drink the boiled
water. He caught the packet of bicarbonate of soda with a
right hook and sent it powdering all over the floor. Bonny,
distraught, walked up and down the kitchen with him and
then sat him on the table while Scott, still clad in his pajamas
and feeling cold, leaned against the radiator.

"You could tell his father," he suggested at last.

Bonny, tearstained herself, was trying to sponge her son's
face.

"If parental involvement is your aim," Scott said, "why not
let him worry with you? After all, Ulysses is Grant's child."

"And you've had a bellyful?"

Scott shrugged but kindly denied it. "Just a suggestion.
That's all."

A good one, Bonny thought. She picked up Ulysses and
made for the door. "I suppose you'll go back to bed now?"
she said over her shoulder. "Your own."

"I was never one to spoil a maiden's chances—or to tarnish the image of motherhood," Scott said.

Maybridge didn't hear Scott Wilson returning to the bedroom next to his. He was sleeping deeply, dreaming that his
son David was marrying Fay and that he was madly jealous.
Meg was Fay's bridesmaid and was wearing her university
gown. The bride, dressed in pink denims, carried a bouquet of
wilting chrysanthemums bound together with fern. The sun
was shining into the church in long streamers of pale yellow
light. Now it was time for the wedding march, and the organ
hadn't enough wind. Someone tried to pump it, and the music
came out in a deep bass speaking voice. It was several
moments before he became aware that the speaking voice
belonged to Dr. Sandy Crofton. "When there's penetration of

the carotid artery," Crofton said, "the blood usually fountains. It didn't."

"Eh?" Maybridge surfaced from his pillow and rubbed his eyes.

Crofton, clad in an ornate dressing gown of dark red silk, repeated what Maybridge obviously hadn't heard. "Someone's done Grant in," he said. "You're needed professionally. Hell of a weekend, isn't it!"

Chapter FIVE

On Sunday mornings, Detective Superintendent Claxby normally played golf with Rendcome, the chief constable. On this particular Sunday morning, the course would have been excellent. The air was crisp and the ground hard. It was the kind of day when even the rough lay back from the ball and let you get at it. And now Maybridge had bunkered him.

Claxby followed him up the stairs to the murder room and refrained from making sour comments. Standing on the threshold of the room, however, Claxby felt his commendable restraint desert him. "What in heaven's name . . . !" His glance at the corpse had been brief; he had seen too many before. What he was looking at in shocked disbelief was the note taped to the headboard. Written in strong capitals with a black felt-tipped pen were the words FAULT THIS MURDER, DETECTIVE CHIEF INSPECTOR MAYBRIDGE, IF YOU CAN.

Maybridge had had time for his own shocked reaction to subside. When he had accompanied Dr. Crofton to the room earlier, he had approached the murder victim in the same manner he approached all murder victims—with his eyes half closed and his stomach churning. Once reconciled to the sight of blood, he became professional, though this time, according to what the doctor was telling him, there wasn't enough— which was an odd but reassuring statement. It was at that point that he had raised his eyes and seen the notice on the bed head, whereupon all queasiness had immediately vanished. Astonishment became rage, and rage became acute embarrassment. Grant lying peacefully dead with arms crossed gently over his chest and with a meat skewer stuck in his neck seemed a mockery, a macabre hoax. It wasn't the sort of thing you believed in. Nobody, but nobody, Maybridge had thought, would carry an act of lunacy this far.

For the last half hour, while waiting for the arrival of Claxby and the forensic team, Maybridge had rehearsed speeches trying to explain the inexplicable. "A thriller writer's little joke?" he suggested bitterly.

"Some joke," Claxby said. He moved over to the bed and looked intently at Grant. His thick white hair was tidy and gleamed as if it had been brushed. The eyes were closed, and his lips formed a tight line. He wore no pajamas, and there was congealed blood around his neck and on his chest. With the skewer penetrating at that angle, one would have expected crimson sheets and even spatters of blood on the ceiling.

Claxby preferred his murders to be normal, not newsworthy. The press would go to town on this one. He pictured the headlines: "Death of Sir Godfrey Grant." "Famous Author Dies in Mysterious Circumstances." "Seminar for Thriller Writers Ends in Death." He looked at Maybridge, imagining a front-page blowup of the note, together with a photograph of the chief inspector and the one word CHALLENGED!

"It's extremely unfortunate," he said, "that you're involved." More like bloody disastrous, Maybridge thought. Claxby, small, sleek, and pedantic, irritated him at the best of times. In these days of drip-dry shirts, he wore separate collars stiffly starched. His suits were invariably gray, and he wore tiepins. He read Proust.

"When you told me you were coming to the seminar,"
Claxby said, "I should have dissuaded you. What in heaven's
name was your lecture about?"

Maybridge gave him a brief outline—the briefest possible.
He wished Claxby would stop invoking heaven. The turbid
realms of hell suited the scene rather better.

He saw with some surprise that Claxby seemed faintly
amused. "It wasn't a very comprehensive lecture," he commented. "What about the spectograph and the spectrometer
—or neutron-activation analysis? You stopped short where
you shouldn't, Tom. Had I lectured, I would have terrified
them with the high degree of forensic detection. No one would
have dared."

He looked around the small cell-like room. "Obviously
single accommodation. Where was Lady Grant's bedroom?"

"Next door."

"How did she take it?"

"Courageously."

Calmly would have been more accurate, though courageously sounded better. He remembered knocking at her door;
she had opened it after a couple of minutes as if she were
awake and waiting for someone. "Oh," she had said, surprised, "it's you!" She had been wearing a green nightdress
with a square neck edged with lace, concealed to some extent
by the forward fall of her long, unbraided hair. He had told
her clumsily that Sir Godfrey had had an accident, that he
was dead. He had intended to try to prepare her for the
shock of what she had to see, but she had pushed past him
swiftly to go into her husband's room. The word accident
had been badly chosen, but he hadn't known how else to put
it. She had stood just inside the door, completely immobile,
and then she had turned back to Maybridge. Her voice was
quite level. "I can't believe it." Maybridge had suggested
brandy or a sedative from Dr. Crofton. "He's not here professionally," she had pointed out. "He doesn't carry drugs in a

little black bag. And I don't want brandy." She had walked
off down the corridor, then to the bathroom. Perhaps she
trembled in there. Perhaps she had cried in there. In ten
minutes, she had emerged, a little paler, perhaps, but very
much in command of herself. "You must have things to do,"
she said. "You'll have to inform the police. Well, of course,
you are the police. I keep forgetting. Thank you for being so
concerned about me. I'm really all right." She had left him
then, saying she had to get dressed, and he had returned to
Grant's bedroom. None of the bedrooms had locks. If you
wanted privacy, you bolted yourself in.

"Who found the body?" Claxby asked.

"One of the young writers—Bonny Harper. Grant is the
father of her son, Ulysses."

"Her son—*who*?"

"Probably an in-joke of some sort," Maybridge said.

"An amusing lot," Claxby observed dryly. "What time was
this?"

"At five-twenty."

"What was she doing in his room at that hour—sex before
six?"

"I shouldn't think so. I could be wrong."

"And how did she take it . . . courageously?"

Maybridge looked suspiciously at his superior officer;
Claxby was no fool. "According to Dr. Crofton, she backed
out of the bedroom and collapsed on the floor."

"Crofton being conveniently around to render help?"
Claxby queried.

"He was returning from the lavatory."

Claxby indicated a syringe and vial on the bedside table.
Diabetic?"

"Yes, according to Dr. Crofton."

"Did the doctor handle the syringe or vial?"

"Not to my knowledge and certainly not while I was in
the room. I asked him if Grant injected himself. He didn't

know, though he thought it highly likely. Grant wasn't his
patient."

"Well, there are three possible answers," Claxby said
gravely. "He accidentally gave himself an overdose, he deliberately gave himself an overdose, or someone else de-
librately gave him an overdose. But have you any theory as
to why a dead man should have a skewer plunged into him
several hours after death?"

Maybridge had been asking himself the same question. It
didn't require a great deal of forensic expertise to know that
someone had pierced an artery that for some while had ceased
to pump. When you saw a lot of dead bodies, you had a fair
idea of the length of time they had been dead. You also had
a working knowledge of anatomy. Certain areas tended to
bleed rather spectacularly, and when they didn't, there had
to be a reason.

"No theory," Maybridge said. Someone had murdered a
corpse, though he wasn't sure if the word "murdered" applied.
It was the first time the situation had been presented to him.
The presenter had also written the note. He took another
look at it. Crisp white typing paper, no smudges of blood. It
must have been taped before he struck. His own words
at the end of his lecture came back to him: "Don't let your
murders be slipshod. Try to make them a fine art." He began
to sweat. There was something particularly revolting about
abusing the dead. Grant's death, by the look of him, had been
peaceful; his features were tranquil. Whoever had pierced
his artery had arranged him neatly, angling his head back just
a little on the smooth pillow before finding just the right area
in his neck. It was obscene.

While the scene-of-crime team worked in the murder room,
Maybridge ordered Dwight Connors to assemble the writers
in the lecture hall. He also asked Connors to provide him with

a full list in duplicate of all the writers present, including their addresses and other occupations, if any. One of these would be run through a computer and checked for any relevant information that might have some bearing on the case. The other would be for reference during the interviews. As he and Claxby mounted the stage, he was strongly reminded of the previous evening. There hadn't been much joy then, either. Grant tended to inspire as much animosity as a nomadic rider raised desert dust. Superintendent Claxby did the talking. Sir Godfrey had been found dead, he told them, but didn't elaborate on the circumstances. A note had been found by his body. A typed version of the note was to be copied by everyone present, using a black ballpoint pen, and the handwriting would then be analyzed by an expert at police headquarters. This would take some time, as would the autopsy, which would be arranged as quickly as possible. As the seminar was scheduled to continue until the afternoon, everyone should carry on as usual but be prepared to be interviewed by Chief Inspector Maybridge and himself. He saw no reason why the preliminary inquiry shouldn't be completed by the end of the day, but it any member had a pressing reason to leave early, then he would give them priority. No one was to leave the premises without his permission. Claxby's manner did not invite contradiction. The writers sat mutely and heard him out.

What Maybridge had to say gave him great pleasure. The scene-of-crime team needed to do approximately an hour's work in the kitchen. In the meantime, breakfast wasn't possible, and no one was to go out for any. This minor revenge was spoiled by Dwight Connors, who immediately stood up and told everyone that there was a coffee machine in the bar and plenty of packets of crisps.

Claxby's humor surfaced. Stymied, he thought, but didn't voice it. Personally, he was glad of the coffee. He hadn't had any breakfast, either, and it was getting close to eight-thirty.

"How did you manage to get them up so early?" he asked
Maybridge. "Did the pack scent blood?"

Connors had raised everyone, and Maybridge didn't know
what he had told them. He was taking the weight of responsibility off Fay. Anything that needed doing, he told
Maybridge, ask him. He would prefer it if she were bothered
as little as possible.

Fay, dressed in a thick brown sweater and slacks, was sitting
next to Cora Larsbury at the front of the hall. She looked as if
she had dressed hurriedly in anything that had come to hand;
there were slippers on her feet. Cora Larsbury was saying
something to her, but she obviously wasn't listening. She
caught Maybridge's eye and looked away. He suggested to
Claxby that if Fay were interviewed first, it would spare her
the strain of waiting. Claxby raised no objection, but his
reason was different. As Grant's widow, she would have to
identify him formally before the autopsy could take place,
and that would take her off the premises for an hour or so.
Death, especially violent death, had its quota of red tape. It
tended to slow up everything.

The interview room was off the hall next to the lecture room.
Until the previous day it had served as Grant's temporary
office. The desk was cluttered with the novice writers' manuscripts, which Claxby pushed irritably to one side. "Fruits of
the imagination. Aconite and belladonna."

"Old-fashioned," Maybridge said. "Murder by insulin."

"Not new, either."

"And not immediately detectable." He hadn't asked Crofton, but the doctor had volunteered the information nevertheless.

Claxby looked in the desk drawer and found a packet of
postcards and some brown manila envelopes. "I won't pretend it wouldn't give me great pleasure for that note to be

copied in your presence," he said, "but that would prove
rather too time-consuming. Sergeant Sayers can see to it.
Arrange it, would you?"

Maybridge, anticipating this, had already installed Sayers
in an adjoining room to await further instructions. He was
careful to avoid looking directly at the sergeant as he explained what had to be done. "Arrange the postcards so that
each person who comes in to copy the note picks a card off
the pile. I want a good set of fingerprints. Get the writer to
place the card in an envelope and write his name on it. Then
get him to lick the flap and seal it down. His saliva might be
useful. When everyone present has copied the note, come and
tell me. You'll then take them back for fingerprinting and
Inspector Barker's analysis."

"He's away, sir," Sayers said, "on a course. Studying Serbo-
Croat in Bath."

"He's been recalled."

Maybridge knew that the big redheaded young sergeant
was holding in his mirth with some considerable difficulty.
He didn't blame him. Barker, though undeniably brilliant,
was a young and bumptious type.

"Any questions, sergeant?"

"How do I get them to come, sir?"

Maybridge had taken a copy of Connors's list and handed
it to him. "Mr. Connors, Grant's secretary and agent, has
listed them. Here's a copy. And don't forget Connors himself.
He'll probably volunteer to fetch the others for you, anyway.
Constable Williams will stay and assist."

Back in the interview room, Maybridge saw that Claxby had
sent out for three red vinyl chairs from the canteen and had
angled one of them so that it faced the window. "A nice cozy
arrangement," he told Maybridge, "a group of three." Cozi-
ness, however, was not Maybridge's aim. The interviews would

be extremely uncomfortable for everyone, including him. The words FAULT THIS MURDER kept ringing through his head like a funeral bell.

"Use your discretion," he told the constable assisting with the interviews. "It doesn't have to be verbatim. Nobody signs anything at this stage. Formal statements will be made later. We just want to get the general picture."

"Superintendent Claxby has already told me that, sir."

"Then I beg your pardon for repeating it," Maybridge snapped irritably.

For the next half hour, before the interviews started, Claxby and Maybridge compared notes and discussed the case. The superintendent asked if there was any animosity to Grant. Maybridge said there was and explained the reasons for it.

"Not a nice fellow, then," Claxby said, "but you know what Cicero said."

Maybridge didn't but was quite sure he was going to be told.

Claxby rolled it out with pleasure. "*'Tacitae maqis et occultae inimicitiae sunt quam indictae et opertae'*," and that translates: Enmities unavowed and concealed are more to be feared than when open and declared."

"Well done," said Maybridge dryly.

Claxby grinned. Maybridge today was very vulnerable, and with good cause. "We'll have all the likely ones first," he said, "starting, as you suggested, with the courageous widow. I'll leave most of the talking to you."

Constable Radwell escorted Fay to the room and then went to sit at the desk, pencil poised eagerly over his notebook. Fay looked at him with some surprise. "You're going to write down what I say?"

"Only anything that's relevant," Maybridge answered for him. He then introduced her to the superintendent, and Claxby made a brief speech of condolence.

"Thank you," Fay answered politely. "I still can't believe

it." She had been eating crisps, and there were some crumbs sticking to the front of her sweater. Maybridge thought that her slippers probably belonged to Godfrey; they were of brown felt and only marginally too big. He remembered her high-heeled patent-leather shoes of the previous evening. She looked far less tense now than she had then. He wondered how she would stand up to the ordeal of the day ahead.

"We need to know where everyone was last night," he told her. "I understand you're tired and shocked, but please bear with us."

"I'm not tired. During the night I slept quite well."

"Even so, you've had the most appalling experience."

"Yes," she said, "I know, but I can't feel it."

Dr. Crofton had told her that such a reaction was normal. A frozen limb felt pain only when the thawing process began, he said, and that could take hours, even days. But she felt neither frozen nor thawed, just indifferent.

Maybridge asked her about Grant's diabetes. She told him he had had it for years.

"Did you assist him with the injections?"

"No, he was peculiarly sensitive about them."

"What do you mean?"

"I walked in on him once when he was injecting himself. He was extremely annoyed, even embarrassed." She frowned, trying to find the right words. "I think he saw his illness as a sort of . . . well, blemish. As if it diminished him in some way. He injected himself in pirvate, usually in the bathroom with the door locked." She looked keenly at Maybridge. "Why? What has his diabetes to do with anything?"

Claxby cut in quickly. "Never mind that now. When we get the pathologist's report later, we'll know what happened. There's no point in conjecture. Did you go to bed about the same time as your husband?"

"No, I went up first. All the bedrooms are single. Mine was next to Godfrey's." She addressed Maybridge. "Does the

superintendent know about the incident in the bar—with
Lloyd, I mean?"

"Yes."

Dwight Connors had told her to make her answers as brief
as possible and not to volunteer any information that wasn't
asked for. She decided not to heed his advice.

"At the time, I didn't know why Lloyd was so upset. I had
done some work on the early chapters of *The Helius Factor*
—just to help out. And when the book was finished, I skim-
med through it to get the general idea. I've never liked his
books, especially not this one. It's too sensational, and the
violence is purely gratuitous. Usually when he was working
on a book, he became withdrawn in a contented sort of way,
but this time he was very edgy and irritable. I think he was
worried that it wouldn't succeed. In many ways, he was unsure
of himself. Most people find that difficult to believe, but it's
true. Critical success mattered to him. It mattered too much.
His career put him off balance; to some extent, it closed off
the real world. It was fortunate that this book did well; he
couldn't cope with failure."

She looked at the two police officers, her expression rather
dazed. "I'm sorry. I was going to tell you about Lloyd. I
don't seem to be able to concentrate."

Maybridge told her to take her time.

She continued after a moment or two. "I avoided reading
several of the later chapters of *The Helius Factor*. That's how
I missed the description of the fire victim. Then someone told
me the pages to look for, and I took the book up to bed and
read them. The description shocked me, made me very angry.
And surprised me, too. Godfrey could be thoughtless and unkind, but I'd never known him to be cruel. What he'd written
was vicious. Anyone knowing Lloyd could see that he'd
modeled the character on him; he hadn't even bothered to
disguise the hood Lloyd wears." She paused, then forced her-

self to continue. "When I heard Godfrey going into his bedroom just before twelve, I went in and told him very bitterly
what I thought of him."

Her candor had made a good impression on Maybridge at
least, who saw her as an Amazonian doing battle on the side
of the weak—an Amazonian who slayed only with words.
Grant had deserved it. Claxby's view was more jaded; he saw
her less fancifully as a woman who had spoken a truth that
could have been damaging. He wondered if she were intelligent
enough to know that her admission was wise. A row in the
privacy of one's home need never be spoken about; in a public
building, there *was* no privacy.

"How did he take it?" he asked.

"The tongue-lashing?" She shrugged. "Surprised at first.
I'm docile most of the time. Lloyd's reaction had shocked him,
too." She frowned and pushed a stray hair away from her
forehead. "What worries me now—now that I'm calm enough
to think about it—is that I might have been harder on him
than I need have been. Writers talk a lot of nonsense about
the subconscious. It was Godfrey's excuse that he hadn't
consciously painted a word picture of Lloyd and that the
whole awful description had been dredged up from somewhere. I didn't believe him, but it could be true. He was
writing about a minor character, as he pointed out to me, and
he was later appalled when he realized what he'd done."

"So he excused himself to you?" Maybridge tried to mini-
mize the row.

"Oh, no—not to me. To himself. He was never abject or
humble. Well, you knew him. He did a lot of shouting back.
I should be more supportive, he told me, not so ready to
accuse. He'd been under a lot of pressure. Hadn't I been
aware of that? Was I so stupid, so obtuse, as to think he'd
deliberately damaged his reputation by writing that way about
Lloyd?" She smiled bitterly. "I said something about the dam-

age to Lloyd being of greater consequence than his reputation . . . And then I walked out."

There was a short silence during which she seemed to be
deep in thought. Maybridge sensed there was more to come.

"About ten minutes later, he knocked on my door. He
wanted the car keys and couldn't find his. I began to be
worried about him; he was in no fit state to drive. Usually,
he was careful not to drink too much, but last night he'd had
a few too many. I asked him where he was going. He said
nowhere. He occasionally smoked cigars, and there was a box
of them in the car. I suppose he thought a cigar would be
soothing."

"So you gave him the keys?"

"He took them from my handbag."

"And then returned later with them?"

"No, he must have gone straight back to his own bedroom."

Maybridge could remember no pungent aroma of cigar
smoke in Grant's bedroom; and it was the kind of smell that
lingered. And he hadn't seen a box of cigars. He wondered
fleetingly if Fay were lying.

He then asked her if she had awakened during the night.
"Yes, I heard Ulysses crying." She turned to Claxby. "Ulysses'
mother, Bonny Harper, was once my husband's mistress.
When the baby arrived, he disowned it. Bonny brought the
baby to the seminar to annoy my husband. But you probably
won't believe me when I tell you it didn't annoy me."

Claxby shrugged noncommittally.

"There are rumors going around that my husband was
mutilated by the skewer after he was dead." She addressed
Maybridge again. "When I looked into the bedroom with
you this morning and saw that note, I thought he had been
murdered. I don't understand."

"Neither do we," Maybridge said gently, "yet. The autopsy
will clear it up for us. He wasn't killed with the skewer. We
don't know how he came to die. But after you've given evi-

dence of identification, the pathologist can get on with the job." He turned to Radwell. "Take Lady Grant to Sergeant Sayers and ask him to arrange transport to headquarters afterward."

Fay paused at the door and spoke with some vehemence. "I'm deeply sorry that this should have happened to you, chief inspector. Whoever wrote that note is a psychopath."

"Possibly."

"It was an excellent lecture. The best we've had from a police officer for a long time."

"Thank you." He appreciated her defense but wished she hadn't spoken quite so warmly in the superintendent's presence.

Claxby, aware of the warmth, watched her curiously as she went out. *La belle dame*, he thought, is wearing men's slippers that are not her husband's. Sir Godfrey's, several sizes larger and of excellent black kid, had been placed neatly at the side of his bed. With whom, he wondered, did the lady dally? Maybridge, he noticed as he returned to his chair, had feet approximately the same size as the deceased's. And that was a relief.

"A pleasant woman," Claxby fished. "Eurasian?"

"Half Indian."

"The marriage, by her own admission, was lukewarm. Had she a lover?"

"I wouldn't know."

"Do you think she cared as little about her husband's mistress as she made out?"

"I'm sorry, but I wouldn't know that, either."

"I'm interested to see the fair Anticleia," Claxby said, "mother of Odysseus. Have her brought in."

"Ulysses," said Maybridge, "and her name is Bonny."

But it was Dr. Crofton who was interviewed next. He put his head around the door. "I'm needed at the hospital."

Claxby told him to come in and close the door. Maybridge introduced them, and Claxby put a tick by his name on the list.

"You're being discreet, I hope?" Maybridge asked. "Lady Grant spoke of rumors. I hope you haven't given anyone out there any details?"

"That's the trouble," Crofton replied soberly. "I haven't said a word out of turn, despite being pestered, but someone has. They know that Grant was already dead when someone skewered him."

"If it wasn't you, and I believe it wasn't, then Bonny Harper? She was the first in the room."

"Bonny would yap about the note," Crofton said, "but her medical knowledge is nil."

"During a murder inquiry," Claxby observed, "everyone yaps. The human race is fascinated by death, especially when it's brutal. It's the yapping that sometimes helps to solve it, though the corpse in the pathology lab usually has the last word."

Crofton, warming to his audience, quoted, " 'Murder, though it have no tongue, will speak with most miraculous organ.' "

Claxby liked a doctor who knew his *Hamlet*. He looked at Crofton with approval. "What's your theory, doctor? How did Grant die?"

Crofton shrugged. "Act of God, perhaps—a coronary. The man was under stress. Lawrence Haydon made a fool of him during the Guillotine presentation. He wasn't exactly popular when Lloyd, minus his headgear, walked into the bar. Grant, in his middle forties, wouldn't be the first to drop dead after going through a period of strain."

"And if his death wasn't natural?"

"No, I can't see him committing suicide. Why should he? I suppose he could have injected himself with an overdose of insulin while drunk or preoccupied and gone into a hypoglycemic coma. The coma would then come on at the earliest about two hours after injecting. I don't know when he injected. Rigor first shows in the face in about five to seven hours after death. I can't say I noticed it, but then, with a ruddy great skewer stuck in his carotid artery, I wasn't looking for it." He grinned at Maybridge. "The note took some of my attention, too."

Maybridge remained silent, resisting an urge to retaliate.

"If he was murdered," Crofton went on, "he was poisoned. My friends out there have used several bizarre poisons in their ghoulish novels, and they're busy swapping theories. Insulin is the current favorite, with curare running a close second. It's obvious and easy. It's injected intravenously. Personally, in my novels, I favor guns." He glanced at Maybridge. "Or let's say I did favor guns—Muriel Slocombe rather bungled the last murder. Thank you for your notes on how to kill by gunfire, by the way. I'll see she gets it right next time."

Claxby, startled, waited for an explanation. Maybridge gave it as an amused Crofton looked on.

"I must admit," the doctor continued, "that on this particular Sunday morning I'm glad your problems aren't mine." He glanced at his watch. "You'll want to ask me questions about my movements last night, I expect. What do you want to know first?"

Claxby took the initiative. "How long have you known Sir Godfrey?"

"About five years. I joined the Golden Guillotine Club at its inception. We've met several times socially and at public functions. He wasn't my patient."

"Did you go to your room last night before or after Grant left the bar?"

"After. I had a scotch with Dwight Connors. Grant went up at about midnight, and I went up shortly after. Connors said something about locking up, so I left him to it."

"How close is your room to Grant's?"

"About five doors away."

"Did you hear anything to cause concern; an argument in his room, for instance?"

Crofton hesitated. "No."

"He and his wife had a row—you didn't hear it?"

"No."

Chivalry? Claxby wondered. He had noticed the doctor's hesitation. "Tell me about Lady Grant."

Crofton showed some surprise. "Fay? Tell you about her? Tell you what about her?"

"How would you sum her up as a person?"

"In one hyphenated word," Crofton said, "long-suffering."

"By her own admission it wasn't a happy marriage."

"Perhaps not," said Crofton brusquely, "but she didn't kill him."

"At this stage we don't yet know if he was killed. All we're sure about is the mutilation. Did you leave your room in the night?"

"Yes, I went to the lavatory just as it was getting light. Bonny's child woke me. He woke most of us."

"Where was the child when his mother left Grant's room?"

"Certainly not with her. Back in the bedroom, I suppose. But Bonny didn't kill him, either," he added.

Claxby tried to be patient. "If someone has an embolism and it reaches the heart or brain with lethal consequences, you accept what has happened as a fact. Police work isn't based on intuition any more than medicine is. If Grant was murdered, anyone on the premises last night could have murdered him. He was mutilated. Anybody could have mutilated him. My mind is open." He turned to Maybridge. "I don't think we need delay the doctor any longer unless there's anything else you want to ask?"

Maybridge shook his head but reminded the doctor to copy the note before leaving for the hospital. Crofton told the superintendent where he could be found and left his telephone number. "I hope you'll have success with the case. I should be interested in the pathologist's report as soon as it's permissible for you to divulge it." Checking an impulse to tell the doctor to mind his own business, Claxby said he would bear the request in mind.

Chapter SIX

Both the superintendent and chief inspector had been fair, Bonny admitted to herself afterward as she made her way up to her bedroom. It had been their duty to question her. They hadn't bullied her, but the nightmare that had been throbbing away in her head, only half believed in, had exploded during their questioning into terrible fact.

Her hands shaking, she bolted the bedroom door. There was a small bottle of scotch in her suitcase, hidden under Ulysses' clean diapers. She poured some into the tooth glass and drank it neat.

Oh, God! she thought. Oh, God!

And that became a mocking Oh, Godfrey!

He had been very easy to mock, a pompous, selfish megalomaniac. But he had been the best lay of her life. His death had been like tearing away a raw lump of herself. That she had been deeply attracted on a physical level she had never denied. And neither had she denied that there had been an answering chord of violence in both of them.

She had explained all this with total honesty. "I could only be violent," she said, "if he was violent back—and then it was mostly verbal. I could never hurt him—I mean seriously hurt him—I couldn't stick a skewer into him when he was lying there—I mean lying there helplessly—I mean . . ."

She gestured wildly, shying away from using the obvious word.

Maybridge had asked her to tell them what she saw when she opened the bedroom door.

She realized he wasn't being sadistic, just professional, and tried to answer calmly. His room faced east and had been lighter than her own bedroom. She had seen him quite clearly, like an effigy in a church, only his hands should have been pressed together in prayer. "I think," she told Maybridge, "that someone had pressed them together and they'd flopped apart."

He had looked mildly surprised but told her to go on.

She had seen something sticking out of his throat—too thin for a knife. It was a kitchen skewer. There was blood. According to rumor, the bleeding had been unnaturally sparse. "For Christ's sake," she had said, snapping at Maybridge, beginning to tremble, "how much blood should there have been? A bathful?"

Claxby asked her if she had gone over to the bed—had she touched Grant? No, she told him, she hadn't been able to move from the doorway. She couldn't remember leaving the room. She remembered crouching outside, her forehead on the cold floor. She didn't remember getting up. She didn't remember anything until she was sitting on the side of her bed and Sandy Crofton had his hands on her shoulders, holding her upright so that she didn't keel over. She had wanted desperately to lie down. She had wanted it to be dark. Ulysses was screaming, but it sounded like screams through cotton-wool.

Claxby had asked her why she hadn't taken Ulysses into Grant's bedroom after coming up from the kitchen with Scott Wilson. "It was your intention, wasn't it, to prod him into parental involvement? Why did you take the baby into your bedroom first?"

She replied contemptuously that Ulysses wasn't a bullet to

shoot Godfrey with. He was a sick baby who needed the warmth of his cot. His father was to go in to see him there.

Maybridge wanted to know if she had opened the cutlery drawer when she was in the kitchen. Had she needed a spoon, for instance, for the bicarbonate of soda?

The seeming banality of the question surprised her. Maybridge explained that the skewers had been kept in the cutlery drawer. Had she seen them? Touched them?

Yes, she said, she'd seen them—and a sharp carving knife. That was a more usual weapon, wasn't it? She hadn't known what she'd touched; her fingerprints were all over everything, probably.

"You earlier had an argument with Grant," Maybridge then reminded her. "He didn't display any affection for his child, so it would be perfectly natural for you to feel some resentment. Exactly what were your feelings when you went into his bedroom?"

"A kind of panic," she tried to explain. "I needed help. He was closer to me and to Ulysses than anyone. Resentment, yes—and spite, too—but more than that. Ulysses was *ours*. Ulysses sick and screaming in the night was *his* problem, too. I needed him then. I needed him in the future. I needed him alive for Ulysses. He has—had—money. I haven't. Ulysses was his only son, acknowledged or not. He could have done things for him. Like a good school. Like a house that isn't the basement of someone else's. Like a holiday now and then. I didn't want him dead. What would be the point?" She had sensed that Maybridge, at least, seemed convinced. But even so, the interview hadn't yet ended. They still had things to ask her.

After Dr. Crofton had returned with her to her room, how long had he stayed with her—five minutes, ten minutes, longer?

She didn't know. She couldn't remember.

What happened then?

He had fetched Sybil Agindale, one of the writers. She hadn't wanted Sybil Agindale. She couldn't stand her. She was flapping around in a panic. She told Sybil to fetch Scott. Scott stayed, and Sybil took Ulysses to her own bedroom to clean him up.

Had Scott stayed with her all night—before Ulysses awoke? Maybridge asked.

Yes, she told him, they had slept together until then.

"A sleeping alibi," Claxby had commented rather acidly.

She had been too traumatized to have any room for anger. That Scott should creep out of her room to mutilate a corpse that had been poisoned was just too ridiculous. And she told him so. Coldly.

Maybridge pointed out that Grant's death might have been natural; he could have had a heart attack.

But she couldn't believe it—his marbled features, the lips almost smiling, the terrible skewer, the blood, the appalling contrast between violence and what looked like peace. It was something she would always remember with horror; natural death didn't take you like that.

She had been making the comparison between natural death and murder—incoherently and close to tears—when Claxby had cut her short. "Thank you," he had said politely but crisply enough to stop her. Maybridge had seen her to the door.

Bonny drank the rest of the whiskey and put the glass down on the floor near Ulysses' cot. It was fortunate that he hadn't seen his father dead. His baby mind wouldn't have understood, but the trauma might have been there. Before the interview, she had left him with Cora Larsbury; now she had a sudden urge to hold him to her. She wanted the feel of him, the smell of him, the sound of him. For his sake now she had to control herself as best she could. She had to be calm.

Downstairs Claxby and Maybridge were discussing the

interview. Bonny had been easy to believe. Emotionally, she was probably capable of killing Grant in a fit of temper, but any act of calculated violence certainly wasn't in character. Bonny Harper wasn't a poisoner or a mutilator. And putting character analysis aside and looking at it from the purely logical point of view, she needed Grant alive. As she herself had told them. Financially, he was—or could have been—an asset.

"Not a strong suspect despite being first on the scene and having ample opportunity," Claxby summed up. Maybridge, meanwhile, wondered just how she had managed to copy the note; during the interview her hands had been shaking badly.

The room was stuffy, and he went over to the window and opened it a little. Bright sunshine was melting the frost on the grass. Cora Larsbury, clad in a thick gray duffel coat, was pushing a small folding pram across the lawn. Its wheels made dark green tracks. Ulysses, now recovering and warmly wrapped up, was just visible under the hood.

"The fussy Sybil Agindale?" Claxby asked, coming over to the window.

"No, that's Cora Larsbury. The most elderly novice, and an expert on Rasputin to boot."

"Nice minds these people have," Claxby observed. "Is she an expert on anything else?"

"She makes sweets."

"What sort of sweets?" Claxby asked, amused. "Chocolates with prussic acid centers?"

"I've no idea."

"Continue in ignorance," Claxby advised, "if only for the sake of your weight."

He decided to summon Scott Wilson. He was supposed to have been in bed with Bonny. He asked if Wilson was a writer, too.

Maybridge didn't know anything about him except that he and Bonny somehow seemed to fit together. "Of the thirty or so here, I only know the ones who were in the running for the award—with the exception of Mrs. Larsbury, who talked to me after the presentation."

"Some race," said Claxby, "and the bloody chop for Grant at the end of it."

As Maybridge didn't have the advantage of knowing Scott Wilson, Claxby asked all the questions. The young man, he thought, presented the usual picture of layabout youth, and he wondered how he had got into bed with the girl without crushing her. She had looked like a stray from a ghetto. He would do well in a rugger scrum. He told him to be seated.

"Before I ask you about the events of last night, Mr. Wilson, I should like to know a little about you. You're a crime novelist?"

"An aspiring one, yes." Scott said.

"Not yet published?"

"We can all dream."

Claxby indicated the pile of manuscripts on the chair by the desk. "One of those is yours?"

"One of those was mine. I removed it last night before Grant could read it."

"Why?"

"Because I didn't think he would be interested in a thesis on Archibald Alison, the eighteenth-century clergyman whose one claim to fame was an essay he wrote on the 'Nature and Principles of Taste' published in 1790."

"You'd better explain what you're talking about."

"Surely." Scott settled himself as comfortably as he could in the hard, straight-backed chair. "My crime novel was called *The Death of Doctor Drummond.* It was in a blue cardboard folder. So was my thesis. When I left home, I picked up the wrong one. I didn't realize what I had done until I came in here to clip on the synopsis. Grant arrived just after I had done so. I hesitated to tell him in case by some mischance he decided to glance through it. His taste is—

sorry, was—pretty execrable. He might have thought the
whole thing deliberate—that I was getting at him. I put
my folder at the bottom of the pile and guided him into a
discussion of his illustrious writing career. It wasn't difficult.
Most people like talking about themselves—Grant more than
most—and later on, when I knew he was elsewhere, I retrieved it."

Claxby looked at Dwight Connors's list. "You're a university graduate with a degree in education?"

"Correct."

"Where do you teach?"

"Nowhere."

"Are you on the dole?"

"That's an old-fashioned way of putting it," Scott said.
"The Department of Health and Social Security doesn't permit
me to starve."

"Obviously," Claxby retorted rather too abruptly. The
young man grated on him. "It also makes it possible for you
to stay at home and write crime fiction."

"Rolling reefers is only marginally more reprehensible,"
Scott agreed cheerfully. "Might I say in mitigation that I have
also tidied gardens for pensioners and cleaned the odd window
or two?"

"You're not here to justify yourself to me," Claxby said
crisply. "You're here to help me solve what could be a
murder."

"So you're not yet sure?"

"We will be. Probably by the end of the day. Now tell
me what you did last night."

"Nothing unique," Scott said, smiling. "You probably did
it, too." He looked at Maybridge, sensing amusement carefully
concealed.

Claxby controlled his temper. "I need to have Bonny
Harper's story confirmed."

"If she told you I slept with her, I did. If she told you I didn't, then I didn't."

"If you're being facetious, you're a fool. If you're being chivalrous, you needn't be."

"Thank you," Scott said. "That's all I needed to know. I slept with her."

"What time did you go to her room?"

"Shortly after one o'clock. I wrestled valiantly with the temptation. A weaker man would have succumbed earlier."

"You hadn't told her you would be visiting her room?"

"No, but the possibility might have crossed her mind; her door wasn't bolted."

"Was she asleep?"

"Yes."

"How long did you stay together?"

"Until Ulysses informed us that he was sick. His mother had almost poisoned him with a prawn. He was very annoyed with her."

The rest Claxby knew, though he put Scott Wilson through it again briefly. "After Bonny Harper decided to inform Sir Godfrey that the child was sick, what did you do? At what point did you leave her?"

"We walked upstairs. She went into her bedroom with Ulysses. I returned to mine."

"You didn't see her going into Sir Godfrey's bedroom?"

"No. It seemed tactful to withdraw."

"When did you know that Sir Godfrey was dead?"

"Shortly afterward—twenty minutes or so. One of the women writers came to say that Bonny wanted me. She then told me why."

"What can you tell me about Sir Godfrey's death?"

"Only what everyone knows. Some joker had stuck a skewer in his throat and written a billet-doux to the chief inspector."

"What else?"

"Again, what everyone knows—he was already dead."

"Have you any theory about how he came to die?"

"A rush of blood to the head after a surfeit of scripts, a surfeit of prawns, a desire to quit this less than successful seminar for a better land far, far away. I really have no idea, superintendent. You tell me."

But Claxby had had enough. He turned to Maybridge. "Have you any questions to ask, chief inspector?"

"Just one," said Maybridge. "How did Dr. Drummond die?"

"Oh, he was pushed off a cliff into the sea"—Scott smiled expansively—"and the awful things happened to his lungs that you told Bonny about. At least we'll all leave this seminar knowing how to commit better murders next time." Maybridge looked at him levelly—and in silence. Scott continued to smile, but even he was beginning to find his own levity a touch wearing. When Claxby dismissed him, he left the room with some relief.

At eleven o'clock, Maybridge and Claxby went into the canteen for coffee. It gave Constable Radwell a break from note taking, and Claxby spent a useful few minutes talking to the kitchen staff, though he thought it highly unlikely that any one of them were involved. They had all been off the premises the previous night by ten and hadn't come on duty until seven-thirty. He thanked them for their patience during the disruptive period earlier in the morning when the forensic team had been in the kitchen; he was glad they had taken the unfortunate affair so calmly. Discretion in a case like this was advisable. The press might become importunate a little later on—as yet they hadn't been informed—and until they were, he would appreciate their continuing discretion. He praised them for the quality of the coffee they served and hoped that they would be able to provide a simple lunch for his officers

—cold meat, perhaps, and a salad? As violent death and a shortage of towels—due to Ulysses—weren't everyday occurrences, they took a little mollifying, but when Claxby put his mind to it, he could be the epitome of charm.

The superintendent returned to the table with a tin of shortbread biscuits. "From the cook," he said.

Claxby's good humor had been restored by Cora Larsbury, who had waylaid them on the way to the canteen. She had recently seen a television program about an Australian funnel spider—or was it tunnel spider? Its bite was lethal, she told them. Had it occurred to the superintendent or the chief inspector that the poison hadn't necessarily been injected. There were other ways. After the abrasive interview with Scott Wilson, her naïveté was refreshing. As far as he knew, he told her, no member of the Golden Guillotine Club was an entomologist, or an Australian. He would, however, bear her suggestion in mind.

"Batty?" he asked Maybridge when she was out of earshot.

"Hard to say."

Claxby remembered his joke with Maybridge about the Larsbury sweets. A Russophile with an interest in antipodean spiders, stuffing chocolates with insulin appealed to him.

"Whoever wrote that note," Maybridge went on, "wouldn't win anything on the intellectual stakes."

"Agreed. But according to Sayers, no one has violently reacted against copying it so far. Why, do you suppose, does he—or she—want to be caught?"

"Masochism?" Maybridge suggested, "or a professional, though misdirected, urge to sample a police cell and then write about it."

"Oh, come," Claxby said, "all they had to do was ask you. Why don't you write them a murderer's handbook—an extension of your lecture between hardcovers at five pounds a time? You could take early retirement." The jibe was irresistible, though Maybridge, who had been expecting it all the morning, ignored it stoically.

There were several writers in the canteen, but their low hum of conversation had no audible undertone of grief. At an adjacent table, the elderly and deaf B. R. Anderson, who dispatched his victim clumsily with a too-short rope, was talking to the school teacher Trevor Martin, who used an acid bath. Did constant mental contact with the macabre blunt their finer feelings? Maybridge wondered. As a child, he had been shocked by a Punch and Judy show—not so much by the story but by the public's reaction to it. In this story, Punch was dead, and the reaction was much the same.

Trevor Martin looked up and caught Maybridge looking at him. He said something to Anderson and came over. He acknowledged the superintendent's seniority by asking him if he might have a word—just a brief one.

Claxby told him to sit down.

Martin looked uneasy and spoke with some hesitation. "I know you intend interviewing me later on, but I think you should be told by me now, and not by somebody else, that I was down in the kitchen during the night. Around three o'clock."

"Oh, yes?" Claxby looked at him keenly. "For what reason?"

"I had a queasy stomach. I suffer from acidity. I needed milk."

"The prawns?"

"No, I didn't touch them. An ulcer. It plays me up at moments of stress. The evening, after the presentation, was upsetting."

"I was in the kitchen about ten minutes," he went on. "I like my milk slightly warmed."

Claxby stirred the dregs of his coffee thoughtfully. "You said that somebody else might tell me that you were up during the night. Who would that be?"

Martin didn't answer immediately, and when he did, it was with some reluctance. "I don't want to cause anyone trouble, and normally I would say nothing—"

"But . . . ," Claxby prompted.

"When I wake at that hour, I don't usually drop off quickly. I needed something to read. I went to the common room to see if there were any magazines or books lying around. Lawrence Haydon was there. The gas fire was on, and he was sitting crouched over it as if he were cold. He saw me coming in. He heard me when I greeted him, but he hardly seemed aware of me. I thought at first he'd had too much to drink; I knew he and his son had gone down to the pub earlier, and he seemed, well, disorientated. I told him I was looking for something to read. He didn't answer. I asked if he were all right, and he said yes—just that, nothing more. I told him that I was pleased he had won the award and that it didn't do to be too sensitive about the circumstances. It was a worthy win, and Grant's letter was nonsense. He didn't say anything. I waited a minute or two—it's difficult to withdraw from a conversation when it touches something rather serious and you expect some sort of response. Conversation is the wrong word, of course; it was more of a monologue. Anyway, that's it. I left him sitting there—and I got the impression that he wasn't drunk at all but deeply distressed."

Claxby thanked him for not holding back information that had obviously worried him. "We shall be interviewing everyone. The pattern will show itself quickly, we hope. Honesty speeds things along."

He was about to question Martin about whether or not he had come across anyone else on his nocturnal wanderings when he was interrupted by Anderson. The old man, uninvited and with his hearing aid whistling disconcertingly, had come over with his chair. "May I join you?" And without waiting for an affirmative, he sat down.

Maybridge offered to get him coffee and then had to repeat

it louder. Anderson declined. He fiddled with his hearing aid. "You'd think in this time of high technology someone would devise something better," he grumbled. "Hearts have pacemakers; kidneys are transplanted. Surely a single hearing device could be inserted permanently in the deep recesses of the ear." He drew the sugar bowl toward him, ran his fingers along the edge of it, and then pushed it away. His movements were restless and his tension obvious. "Grant," he said after the awkward pause, "is much maligned. I've known him for years. We used to walk sometimes in the Quantocks. He was a man of some sensitivity. A nature lover. We talked together a great deal. He was always generous with his time and attention. My deafness never exasperated him. He spoke clearly and slowly. And he listened to me. If I had a problem with my book, we would talk it over. His criticisms were honest. He always went to a lot of trouble with the novice writers' manuscripts. He knew what he was talking about and would help an aspiring writer to the best of his ability. Though God only knows why he should have bothered. He was at the top of his own particular tree."

Safe in his deafness from untimely interruption, he went on. "I believe his criticism of the Haydon book was just, if rather unfortunate. Had he been wise, he wouldn't have made it, but he made it in good faith and not out of malice. He wasn't a malicious man. And the description of the burned victim—that's the sort of hazard any writer might come up against. You write fiction, and then someone tells you it's fact and slams a libel action on you." He looked at the two police officers. "You'll hear a lot of derogatory comments about him —based on jealousy. I'm trying to set the record straight. That's all."

Speaking slowly and clearly, Claxby told Anderson that the police were not biased and that he and Maybridge had open minds. But that he should play Antony to Grant's Caesar was interesting. A defense springing from honest liking, he wondered, or a reaction to guilt? And Maybridge, silent throughout the exchange, was wondering the same. The friendship between the two men was difficult to imagine. He hadn't seen any evidence of it during the seminar; they hadn't even gotten together in the bar last night. There was about twenty years' difference in age, and their personalities seemed incompatible. Their books, too, were in marked contrast. Grant's fiction was vigorous—or what he'd seen of it, anyway—whereas the one book of Anderson's he'd read had struck him as sad and rather sordid. Anderson would have been old in youth —there was no sparkle to him; he possessed the sharp, uncomfortable gleam of nerves stretched tight.

His eulogy of Grant had been delivered a few decibels above normal; now suddenly his voice was low and laced with venom. "The uncaring bitch!"

Maybridge, startled, followed his gaze and saw that Fay had come into the canteen with Dwight Connors. She was wearing a light blue tweed coat with high-heeled black shoes and had probably just returned from making the formal identification of her husband. She seemed very composed and paused to speak to a group of writers seated at a table near the door while Connors went ahead and found an empty table. He waited until she joined him and then went to collect two cups of coffee. When he returned, she tasted the coffee and made a grimace of distaste. He was about to get up again, but she put a hand on his and stopped him. She went over to the counter and found a bowl of sugar. Returning to the table, she knocked the bowl accidentally against the corner of the counter. It broke, and the sugar spilled on the floor. She looked at it, smiling. The smile became a laugh. And then she bent over in pain as her laughter burst into weeping.

Connors was at her side. He didn't touch her. Maybridge felt distinctly uncomfortable; to look at them was an intru-

sion. He glanced at Claxby and guessed what his colleague
was thinking. It hadn't been an overt relationship, but now
it was quite unmistakable.

"A nice performance," Anderson said contemptuously.
"She's been cuckolding her husband for years."

Chapter SEVEN

Kate was walking around the perimeter of the croquet lawn in the bright morning sun. Her limbs felt heavy, and she moved like a geriatric. Ulysses, released from the confines of his pram, was sitting on a folded rug. His cheeks were a bright pink, and he was chortling happily as Scott Wilson gently rolled croquet balls toward him. His mother, leaning against the door of the shed where the games equipment was kept, watched him glumly. Kate passed close by, and though Bonny said, "Hi!" in greeting, she didn't answer.

Kate's interview had lasted less than a half hour and had followed the course she had expected it to take. They had wanted to know about her nursing career. As a community nurse, what were her duties? Visiting patients' homes, she had told them, giving any care that might be needed. She had looked at Claxby with a touch of bravado. "Injecting insulin."

The superintendent strongly resembled one of the consultants in the burns unit who had come to speak to her shortly after Lloyd had been taken to intensive care. He had told her gravely that the prognosis wasn't good, that the scarring would be severe. Cocooned in shock, she had seemed to hear him across an abyss, her mind in a turmoil of terror. He had looked very spruce. There was a signet ring on his little finger. He hadn't smelled of fire. His hair wasn't singed. There was no blood on him. Had his skull been split open, it would have shown a computer, very neat, very efficient. He had given her a lecture on third-degree burns, and she had thanked him politely. Superintendent Claxby was a man cast in the same mould. He did his job with cool professionalism. She felt depersonalized in his presence, like a bacterium under a miscroscope. And Maybridge, too, had distanced himself. Last night he had shown considerable sympathy. Today he treated her with polite reserve.

Information had been extracted subtly—the supportive role she played in the marriage and writing partnership; her anxiety the previous evening during Lloyd's absence; her own absence from the room immediately prior to his return; her resentment of Grant. And by the end of the interview she felt as weak as if she had donated two pints of blood.

There was a green-painted summerhouse beyond the croquet lawn. She needed to sit there alone for a while to ease her turmoil. But it wasn't until she had walked around to the sunny side of it that she noticed that Cora Larsbury was already there. Too late to back off with an excuse, Kate went to sit beside her.

Cora was sitting on a folded mackintosh, and she moved over so that Kate could share it. The bench was damp, and Cora suffered from rheumatism. "I saw you go in for the interview," she said, "and I saw Lloyd waiting outside. I didn't see him in the canteen for either breakfast or morning coffee." With unusual tact, she didn't ask Kate how the interrogation had gone, nor did she comment on her appearance. The young woman, she thought, looked perfectly dreadful.

Kate, deliberately avoiding Cora's compassionate gaze, noticed that a ball of wool had dropped by her feet and was getting dirty. She picked it up and put it in the old woman's holdall near a tin of cream toffees. Aware that an answer was required of her, she gave it. "I brought him breakfast on a tray."

She had taken him a cup of tea earlier and had broken the news of Grant's death to him. Still hung over from the previous night, he had frowned up at the ceiling for a moment or two before responding. If he were surprised or shocked, he didn't show it. His head ached, he told her at last, as if that were most important. Where were the bloody aspirins? She had found them for him and told him brusquely that he had better get up; the police were holding an inquiry. He would meet Maybridge if he had to, he said, but no one else. She had explained with cold patience that he had no choice. "Your mutilation, compared with Grant's, is trivial," she had said, regretting the words as soon as they had been spoken.

Maybridge, during the interview, had asked her if Lloyd had needed psychiatric help to come to terms with his disfigurement. She had admitted that he had but that he was now discharged. The doctor, she stressed, was satisfied that he was now emotionally stable and able to cope with his trauma. Claxby asked if she agreed with the doctor. She said she did and hoped it sounded convincing. Lloyd's mental stability was very precariously balanced; God knew what he had done while she was asleep.

"You have been an exceptionally good wife," Cora said gently. "At times it can't have been easy."

"With half his face burned away, it wasn't easy for Lloyd, either."

Cora took the tin of toffees from her holdall and prized off the lid. "Have one. I made them." Kate shook her head. Cora helped herself.

An airplane appeared as a swift flash of silver high up in the sky before entering a cloud. The faint hum of its engine

became louder and then faded away. It merged silently on
the far side of the cloud. Cora watched it until it disappeared.

"There are different forms of freedom," she said. "A flight
to a dream holiday, perhaps—or just freedom inside your
head. Our freedom—yours, Lloyd's, and mine—is in our
writing. We all have scars, though they don't always show.
When the real world gets particularly nasty, we can escape
from it. We're lucky."

"Lucky?" Kate asked sharply, the word exploding out of
her with pain.

"Yes," Cora insisted. "Lucky. Put a bad situation into print
and it gets better. Push it on to a character, let the character
carry the burden for a bit, and it eases. What happened to
Lloyd was awful, but he's still young enough and clever
enough to turn it to some good." She flipped the toffee paper
onto the grass, then had second thoughts and retrieved it.
"Lloyd has time on his side," she continued. "I haven't, and
that I resent. I've always wanted to make my name with a
book. It's my greatest ambition. Even now, at seventy, I'd
gladly give years away to succeed." Her eyes filled with
tears. "I mean it. It's all I have to hang on to. You and Lloyd
have published. Critics have given you good reviews. I envy
you both with all my heart. Just tell Lloyd that."

To hell with books, Kate thought, surprised by the out-
burst. She wondered what Lloyd was telling the police officers.
She wished she could get inside his head and speak for him.
Have a care, my love, she thought. They're out to get you.

"Who do you suppose did it?" Cora asked, calm again.

Kate shrugged. Fear for Lloyd had her suddenly by the
throat, and she was unable to answer.

Maybridge had given Claxby prior warning of Lloyd's appearance, but even so, when the superintendent saw him for the
first time, he was disturbed. If I looked like that, he thought,
and Grant described me in a book, I'd be tempted to dispatch

him, too. Of them all, Lloyd Cooper had the strongest motive for a senseless and repulsive act of violence. Pity momentarily overrode all other emotions, although true to form, he tried not to let it show.

There was a marked contrast in the attitudes of husband and wife toward the questioning. Kate had answered everything in a low monotone and given the impression, unwittingly, of being extremely bored. Maybridge had seen that reaction many times before and wasn't deceived by it. Stress affected people differently. Take Fay's breakdown in the canteen that morning. With Lloyd, it showed in a jauntiness of manner, a kind of feverish flippancy.

"Thank you for getting me to bed last night," he said. He turned his chair so that he had his back to the window. "For your sake," he said to the superintendent, "not mine."

Claxby, embarrassed, didn't know what to say, so Maybridge, to cover the silence, told him about the Chester Barrington novel.

"My book—or rather, our book—" Lloyd said, "fell down on the more advanced fingerprinting techniques. In this murder, you should have no difficulty. A good calligraphist—or even a mediocre one—plus prints on the paper and you're home and dry."

"Murder?" Claxby asked.

"According to my wife, yes. She tells me that's the general opinion." After leaving his bedroom, he had carefully avoided everyone. Contact with the sergeant earlier that morning as he copied the note had been trauma enough.

"But what motive?" Claxby asked, now finding it a little easier to look at Lloyd and beginning to relax.

"Keep looking," Lloyd invited. "Shall I move into a better light? Tell me, superintendent, is there a better motive than this?'"

"It had occurred to me," Claxby admitted. "I was told of Grant's description in his book."

"But it didn't occur to you." Lloyd turned to Maybridge. "I could hardly walk up the stairs—remember? You and Connors had to undress me. Rumor has it that Grant was poisoned. That requires delicate manual control of ampoules and syringes. I couldn't even control my piss."

He rubbed his eyes with his fists. His eyelids were burning, and his head still throbbed. The aspirins Kate had given him weren't working.

Maybridge resisted the temptation to point out that only relative sobriety was needed to plunge in the skewer. And it fell to Claxby, dutiful as always, to ask the necessary question.

"You might have thought you had good cause to mutilate Grant. You might have been sober enough to control your hand for that—and drunk enough to want to do it. Did you?"

"The thought appeals to me," Lloyd said. "I wish I had skewered the bastard."

"Why should Grant have pilloried you in his book?" Claxby asked with uncomfortable directness.

"Because he's a sadist?" Lloyd suggested, "or is that too simple?"

"Was there enmity between you for any reason?"

"I hardly knew him."

"He referred to it, obliquely and apologetically, on the stage during the award ceremony," Maybridge said. "Did your wife tell you?"

Kate hadn't. Her silence had in fact been of almost Trappist dimensions; after telling him of Grant's death and the general reaction to it, she had hardly spoken at all.

"No."

"I can't remember his exact words," Maybridge said, "but he suggested that certain events are buried in the subconscious, that scenes from the past sometimes surface and seem to be new material."

"And you believe that?"

"When he said it, he was looking at the empty chair next to your wife, where you would have been sitting. He seemed to believe it."

"He could have been excusing Lawrence Haydon's so-called plagiarism."

"No. In retrospect, I'm fairly positive that he was referring to you."

Lloyd examined his beautifully kept hands. "You're also fairly positive that I went down to the kitchen last night, removed a skewer, went to Grant's bedroom, found him dead, and was so incensed that someone else had beaten me to it that I carved his obituary regardless." He smiled. "I'm sorry you should have been taunted by a psychopath, chief inspector. You don't deserve to be. But you'll know soon enough that *I* didn't write that note. At some stage I suppose you'll take scrapings of my fingernails, and they'll prove negative, too."

"All the same," Claxby said, "it pleases you that Grant is dead."

"That I don't deny."

"A few minutes ago you talked of poison, mentioned ampoules and syringes. Why?"

Lloyd shrugged. "I don't know. Arsenic in his Ovaltine, perhaps?"

"Have any of the characters in your books been poisoned?"

Lloyd seemed amused. "Life imitating art? Of course several characters have been poisoned—and stabbed and strangled and electrocuted. In the one before the last one, I used phenol on my victim. That's injected, too."

"What do you think happened in this case? Assuming, of course, that he didn't die from natural causes?"

"He was a diabetic, so an overdose of insulin springs immediately to mind."

"How would it have been administered?"

"As a crime writer, I'd suggest that a stronger form of insulin was substituted at some time during the evening."

"Can you think of anyone with access to insulin who might be attending the seminar and have a motive?"

It took a couple of minutes for the significance of the question to register. Had his head been clearer, it would have taken less. Maybridge felt some compassion. Claxby's thrust had drawn blood emotionally, though at this stage of the interrogation it was scarcely justified. They were still very much in the dark.

Lloyd spoke quietly and slowly, forcing the words out. "That's my theory as a crime writer. In the ordinary world, things are simpler. He probably took an overdose of insulin, accidentally or intentionally."

"Accident or suicide—but not murder?"

"No."

"And yet when you came in," Claxby said silkily, "you seemed quite positive that it was."

Lloyd remained silent, unable to reply to the taunt. His face seemed to have thinned and aged in a matter of minutes.

"I can't remember whether or not I reminded your wife to copy the note," Claxby went on. "If she hasn't, would you ask her to go along and do so straightaway?"

He stood up, terminating the interview. Kate Cooper, he was quite sure, wouldn't have wasted her time with a meat skewer. Her methods would have been more professional.

Lloyd looked at Maybridge much as a drowning man looks for a rope in a turbulent sea. Maybridge looked away.

Kate had made her escape from Cora and was walking through the car park when Lloyd caught up with her. For a brief mad moment he felt like pushing her into their Austin and driving fast and far in any direction away from there. Instead, he just touched her hand, then held it. It was very cold. "You shouldn't be out-of-doors without your coat."

He rarely made that sort of contact. They hadn't held hands for a long time. Their sexual relationship was good, but apart from bed, they didn't touch very much. She sensed his concern for her, and this, too, was new. Whether he was cold or hot, in pain or slighted, embarrassed or hurt, had been her concern for years. Before they began having success with their books, she had listened to his complaints about the jobs he didn't like. When he threw them over, she didn't chide him. When the books made money, they shared the fun. When they didn't, she went out nursing. She was strong Kate, practical Kate, loving Kate.

Just how loving is she? he thought, fondling her fingers. Loving enough for *that*? The cold morning air seemed to get inside his clothes and lie like frost on his skin.

"They asked me to remind you to copy the note." He spoke quietly.

"I've already done it."

"And I."

He had copied it before going in for the interview and with some degree of amusement. But there was nothing amusing about anything any more. He spoke his thoughts aloud. "The downward spiral."

"What?" She wondered if he were not yet sober.

"Since the fire, life has been squalid—especially for you."

Sorry for her. Not for himself. That was new. But this was no time for a reassessment of things gone. She felt incapable —mentally and emotionally—of coping. All she wanted was to walk alone in the grounds and know some sort of peace. She removed her hand.

As they walked back to the house, she asked him about his interview.

"They think I probably mutilated Grant."

Kate thought it likely, too; and likely that he wanted to be caught. There was a trace of masochism in his psychosis. His performance last night in the bar, although extreme, had been in character, too.

Lloyd waited for a scathing comment. She didn't make it.

He wanted to tell her that he loved her. Had her hand remained in his, he might have done so. He hoped that she understood that he did. He was terribly frightened for her. That they were equally suspect in each other's eyes occurred to him. He didn't know what to do.

Claxby and Maybridge were studying the notes taken by Constable Radwell during the Cooper interviews.

"They would have been acting independently, of course, and unknown to each other," Claxby suggested. "If she had wanted to send Grant to kingdom come, she could have done so very effectively by inducing a hypoglycemic coma. She has the medical know-how. Perhaps when he came upon the corpse later, he guessed what his wife had been up to and tried to draw suspicion away from her by performing the mutilation."

Maybridge dismissed the idea. The possibility that Grant could have been killed by Kate had only just occurred to Lloyd during the interview. He had been visibly shaken. Apart from that, he was no fool, and as a professional crime writer, he wouldn't make the elementary mistake of thinking the autopsy wouldn't reveal the true cause of death.

"All this is so much shadowboxing," Claxby complained irritably. "I find it a great deal more exhausting than thumping suspects with facts. Have we murder dressed up in a respectable shroud, have we suicide, or have we natural causes, pure and simple? All we're certain of is the mutilation."

Maybridge took out his pack of cigarettes and lit up. "By now Langridge will be removing the shroud. We should have the answer soon."

"You're heading for cancer," Claxby warned him. "If Langridge ever does an autopsy on you, he'll home straight in on your lungs."

"Nice and easy for him," Maybridge said, unruffled.

Claxby studied the list of names that Dwight Connors

had given him. He had written his own name at the bottom and next to it had entered his profession as private secretary and literary agent. But Connors, Claxby decided, could wait. The name typed just above his was Christopher Haydon, pharmacist. Here, as in the case of Kate Cooper, there was both motive and access. He asked Constable Radwell to send for him, but then Maybridge intervened. "I don't think he's on the premises. He wasn't even expected to stay for dinner last night. I'm fairly sure he didn't stay overnight."

"Then we'll see his father, the infamous plagiarist."

"Alleged," Maybridge pointed out dryly. "He's an elderly retired major with a lot more writing talent than Grant."

"Yours is the invidious position," Claxby reminded him. "Someone out there wrote you the note—remember."

"I'm not being sympathetic."

"Good," Claxby said. "And keep it that way," he added, thinking about Lady Grant.

Lawrence Haydon, with the help of Dwight Connors, was digging a hole behind the sports-equipment shed. It wasn't an ideal position for a grave, but there wasn't anywhere else. The croquet lawn couldn't be disturbed, and though rotting flesh might be of some use in the vegetable garden, organic material was more aesthetically acceptable when processed and packaged. And as Connors had pointed out rather flippantly, it wouldn't do for Marcus to be dug up with the cabbage.

Dwight Connors had never owned a dog. As far as he knew, you put the dead body in a plastic bag and gave it to the garbageman. But he hadn't liked to suggest this method of disposal to the major, who was clearly still very upset. The old man hadn't gone down to breakfast and had been sitting on the side of his bed in a state of frozen grief when one of the writers had looked in on him and then explained the scenario to Connors, which was why he was here now.

His spade cut into the nettle-covered soil with some viciousness. He wanted to be with Fay. After her breakdown in the
canteen, he had taken her to his bedroom and sat her down
in the easy chair by the window. They had sat together for a
long time, not saying anything but drawing comfort from
each other. She had got up eventually, saying there were
things she had to do. The bloody seminar, he had told her,
could run itself. Her responsibility, in any case, was over.
It was in the hands of the police. "In the kind hands of Chief
Inspector Maybridge," she had said, like a little girl who
would believe anything. Maybridge wasn't in the business of
being kind, or unkind, he had snapped irritably. He was
looking for an arrest.

"There's clay this end," Lawrence Haydon complained. Years
ago he'd had muscles like Connors. He'd been middle-aged,
optimistic, and living with a wife who had provided pleasant
companionship. Latterly, he'd had Marcus. Like a great many
lonely retired people, he had needed another living presence
—something to talk to, something to love. Now he had
nothing. He was old. He was sick. His breathing threatened
to choke him when he wielded the spade, and he bitterly
regretted having come to the seminar. Christopher's plan had
been stupid and extremely incriminating. He should never
have agreed to it. It was fortunate, under the circumstances,
that he hadn't given Grant the box as planned. He would
have to deny strenuously for both their sakes that it had ever
existed. He made another abortive effort to dig and leaned
heavily on the spade. It was all too much. By now, Connors's
side of the grave was several feet deep. He went over to
Haydon's end to help. "Why didn't you make sure the bedroom door was secure when you left the dog in your room
last night?" He hadn't intended to sound censorious. He was
truly sorry that the animal was dead.

"It was secure. Someone let him out."

He and Christopher had returned from the Golden Hart shortly after eleven. Christopher's car was awkwardly parked by the stables at the back of the building, so they had used his Fiat. Christopher had wanted to drive it, but Lawrence wouldn't let him. The car was new, and Christopher tended to crash the gears. Afterward, his head muzzy with whiskey, he had also insisted on driving it back. Marcus had loomed out the hedge near the main gates and been dazzled by the headlights. The car hadn't stopped in time. A younger dog might have survived the impact, but Marcus was twelve, slow and frail. The old man had gone on his knees and cradled the old dog, holding his head for the few minutes it took him to die. Afterward, he had taken off his mackintosh to use as a shroud, and Christopher had helped lift the dog onto the backseat of the car. All this had been done in silence; grief had struck them dumb, and it wasn't until they had driven up to the parking ground that anguish was expressed in words. He had planned to drive home with Marcus in the morning. Now morning was here, and no one was allowed to drive home.

"You should never have brought him," Dwight said with a touch of impatience.

"I had no one to leave him with."

"You didn't bring him to the seminar last year."

"He stayed with my son. Christopher drove to Weston for the weekend."

Dwight didn't point out that that would have been a better arrangement this year. Neither the dog nor the son should have been on the premises, but filial support under the circumstances was understandable and excusable. He looked down into the hole and decided it was deep enough. "Shall I lift him in for you?"

The shape of the dog was clear under the beige mackintosh. Rigor was fully established. Last night the body had been limp and easier to move. Lawrence suggested they should

take an end each. He put his hand under the mack and
stroked Marcus's head. The hair was soft, the muzzle hard
and cold like a steel ball. Before Connors took his end,
Lawrence slipped the belt around the body to keep the mack
in position. He wished he could have managed all this on his
own. After the accident, Christopher had wanted to stay the
night, but he hadn't let him. He wanted him gone. Other
people at a time like this were an intrusion. You had to talk
to them; you had to pretend to be tougher than you were.
He had planned to bury Marcus under the cherry tree in the
garden at home. He hadn't wanted him laid to rest here, but
there was no knowing how long the police might be with the
interrogations.

Marcus dead was heavier than Marcus alive, or seemed to
be. It was like lifting a solid wedge of wood. With some difficulty, they lowered him awkwardly into the hole.

Dwight thought it was a waste of a good mackintosh; some
old sacking would have done, but he was wise enough not to
say so. The major, standing stiffly with his spade at his side,
looked like someone attending a military funeral. A few shots
over the dog's head and the sounding of the last post, Dwight
thought, would terminate the whole sorry business in a
manner befitting the major's grief. Together they began
shoveling on the soil. And it was at that stage that Constable
Radwell came upon them. He asked them what they were
doing.

"Burying Marcus," Dwight volunteered. The major was too
upset to speak. "A dog," Dwight explained, noticing the
constable's expression.

Radwell, an animal lover, was sympathetic. He waited
patiently until the dog was buried and the soil stamped down,
then led the major back to the interview room. With some
sensitivity, he asked him to wait outside while he went in to
apologize for the delay and to explain the reason for it.

Claxby was irritable. "What were you doing—performing the last rites?"

"I couldn't hurry him, sir."

"Obviously you didn't try."

Lawrence Haydon gave the impression of a man who would have faced a firing squad with supreme indifference. Even welcomed it. He couldn't envisage his life in Weston without Marcus. He didn't want to go back there. Or stay here. He felt suspended in a gray area where there was no warmth of human contact and where the sun never shone. He sat down and crossed one muddy shoe upon the other, waiting in silence.

Maybridge said he was sorry about the dog. And meant it.

Haydon shrugged.

"How did it happen?"

"My reflexes aren't as good as they used to be. Marcus was dazzled by the headlights. I couldn't stop the car in time."

Maybridge thought of the large golden retriever. He and Meg had once owned a similar one. "Weren't you taking a risk letting the dog out at night?"

"I didn't let him out. Grant did."

But there were limits, Maybridge thought, to believable villainy. That Grant could accuse Haydon of plagiarism was believable; that he could model a character on Lloyd Cooper was believable; that he could make love to Bonny and sire her child was believable; but that he should creep along a corridor and spitefully let a dog out somehow was not. Unless the dog had been barking or howling or making a general nuisance of himself. He tentatively suggested that this might be the reason, but Haydon denied it. "I had walked Marcus on the grounds before shutting him in my bedroom. I left him asleep in his basket, one I bought specially for him before coming here. Grant let him out."

"But why?"

"Obviously in the hope that he might be killed."

Claxby took over. "At about what time did you get in last night?"

"My son and I drove back from the Golden Hart just after closing time. We arrived on the grounds of St. Quentin's at around about eleven and after the accident stayed on the grounds a little while. Marcus took about five minutes to die. It took a while longer for me to understand that he was dead. Christopher and I lifted him into my car, and we drove up to the front parking ground. We remained in the car."

"Did you see Grant last night when you did go in?"

"Yes, he was coming out of the bar. I accused him of letting Marcus out of my bedroom. He denied it."

The argument had been short and bitter. The wretched animal shouldn't have been on the premises, Grant had said, but he'd had nothing to do with letting it out.

"Did anyone overhear your conversation?"

"My son was with me. I began to feel ill. Grant suggested I should go to my room and calm down. I have a heart condition," he added.

"You felt very angry toward Grant?"

"Naturally."

"Did you go to your room?"

"I stood in the hall and waited until Grant went down the corridor toward the kitchen. I wasn't sure that I could climb the stairs. I didn't want him to see me trying, so I sat on a chair in the hall until I could breathe more easily. Then I went up to my room and lay down on the bed."

"Fully clothed?"

"Yes. My son brought me up some brandy."

"How long did he stay with you?"

"Until I felt better. He wanted to stay the night. But as there were no available bedrooms, it would have meant his sitting in the chair. I told him it wasn't necessary. There was nothing he could do about me or Marcus or anything. So I told him to drive home."

"Where is his home?"

"London."

"So he left you?"

"Reluctantly, yes."

"Did you then undress and get into bed?"

"No, I stayed in the same clothes all night."

"Why?"

"Because I needed to go out again."

Claxby glanced over to Maybridge and then carried on with the questioning. "For what reason?"

"I was worried about Marcus. He was on the backseat of the car. I couldn't remember if I had locked it or not."

Maybridge interposed gently, "But the dog was dead."

"I needed to see him."

"To be sure he was dead?"

"No, to be sure he was lying quietly and comfortably in death."

Haydon's eyes looked haunted. He had had mad visions of predators clawing at the corpse, pulling it from the car, hurting it. Whiskey, brandy, and despair had made him less than rational. This morning he was sober, but even more despairing.

Claxby asked him what time he had gone down to see the dog, but Haydon couldn't say. The night had been one long vast tunnel of black. If clocks ticked, he hadn't heard them. And if babies cried, he hadn't heard them, either.

Claxby snapped that he wasn't helping the investigation, or himself, very much. "Was there anyone else on the grounds when you took your walk outside?"

"I don't know. I didn't see anyone."

"You say you used the front parking ground?"

"Yes. It's usually full. But last night it wasn't."

"What did you do when you returned to the building?"

"I was cold. I went to the common room and lit the gas fire."

"Do you remember speaking to Trevor Martin when you were sitting in there?"

"Yes. He made one or two pompous remarks about my book. However, I was in no mood to converse with him."

Trevor Martin had pinpointed the conversation at about three o'clock. Claxby wanted it confirmed, but Haydon remained determinedly vague.

"How long did you stay in the common room after Trevor Martin left you?"

"Until I felt warmer."

"How long was that?"

"I don't know."

"Did you stay there all night?"

"No, I went back to my bedroom. Eventually."

"When you went back to your bedroom, was it dark, or was dawn breaking?"

"It was dark."

"Before going back to your bedroom, did you go anywhere else? The kitchen, for instance?"

"No."

"Did you at any time go into Grant's bedroom?"

"No."

"You know, of course, what happened to Grant last night?"

"I know he died, superintendent. If I were capable of feeling anything remotely resembling joy, then I would feel it now. As it is, I don't feel anything."

"Important as your own emotions are to you," Claxby said nastily, "could you project your thoughts outward and on to the main issue. Can you tell me anything about Grant's death?"

Lawrence Haydon answered with dignity. "I didn't kill him. I wish I had."

"Could you have mutilated him?"

"With great pleasure."

"And did you?"

"No."

Claxby turned to his colleague. "Well?"

Maybridge was remembering his conversation at dinner with Christopher Haydon the previous evening. "Your son was telling me that a large quantity of drugs had been stolen from his premises. I omitted to ask him how long ago this occurred. Do you happen to know?"

"I've no idea. In what way is it relevant?"

Maybridge pressed on, anxious to glean something from the interview. "Does your son live on the premises?"

"Yes, he has a flat over the shop. Why?"

"Have you ever stayed with him?"

"Once or twice. But not recently. I've no knowledge of chemistry. I couldn't offer practical help. Are you suggesting I might have stolen them?" The lines of grief softened; Haydon looked almost amused.

"What did you do in the army?"

"As a professional soldier, I killed people—reluctantly, infrequently, and a long time ago. I didn't poison my enemy. I shot him. It was all very negative."

"But your attitude toward Grant wasn't negative."

"Would yours be—under the circumstances?"

"Last night, at the Guillotine presentation, toward the end of your speech, your son came over to the stage. He had a small box in his hand. I think he was about to give it to you, but you hurried him away. What was in it?"

Haydon's eyes narrowed slightly. "I can't recall any box."

"It was about half the size of a shoe box—gray cardboard with a lift-up lid. I'm quite positive he had arranged to give it to you."

Haydon was becoming agitated. "Had the occasion been happier, it might have been a gift."

"Was it?"

"I didn't see it."

"All right. Assuming you didn't, what might have been inside? What was this 'gift'?"

"A pair of dueling pistols," Haydon suggested bitterly, "or better still, a Luger—or a small incendiary. You must have sensed the atmosphere as well as everyone else, chief inspector. Use your imagination."

"In my profession," Maybridge said smoothly, "we exercise our imagination as little as possible. We deal in facts. I know your son had a box, and I know he intended giving it to you. You didn't let him. I believe you know what's in it."

Haydon felt a tightness across his chest and began to sweat. "I don't know what you're talking about."

Maybridge felt he couldn't force it any further. Later, perhaps. The major had spoken of a heart condition, and he was ominously pale.

"Have you anything more to tell us?"

"Nothing."

Both Maybridge and Claxby decided to let him have the last word.

Chapter EIGHT

Dwight Connors still had smears of mud on his jeans and on the sleeve of his jacket when he was called to the interview room. He had been on his way to the bathroom when he had come across Fay by the telephone in the hall. Still pale and red eyed from weeping, she was holding the receiver as if she were welded to it by an electric current. "Gina needs to be told," she said, "and I can't do it."

He had taken the receiver from her gently. "You'll probably need permission from the police. The press haven't been informed yet."

"Dammit, she was his first wife—she's the mother of his twin daughters—she has the right to know."

"She'll know later. Don't take that burden on yourself."

In an ideal world, he thought as he took the chair facing the two police officers, there would be no trauma. He and Fay would lead lazy, quiet, nonsocial lives. They would sit in sweet-smelling gardens and bathe in nonpolluted seas. They would have children strong in limb and intellect, and the wreckers, as dead as Marcus, would be buried deep in lime.

Claxby spoke first. "Tell me about Grant."

Dwight had come to the interview room with the firm intention of throwing up protective verbal barriers around Fay; the less she came into the conversation, the better. A

115

dissertation on Grant's work was as good a block as any, especially since he had decided to dispel a few myths.

"He could probably be best described as a supreme self-publicist," he told the superintendent. "I'm not denigrating his writing talent by saying that. His early books were very successful. Latterly, though, he wasn't doing very well. Although these seminars gave him the chance to parade around as the archetypal best-selling author generous with advice and patronage, the truth was rather different. His sales were flagging, and it worried him. He didn't need the money, but by God, his ego needed the success."

Aware that his tone was too critical—especially under the circumstances—he tried to soften it. "Most writers have periods of difficulty; they tackle the problem in different ways. So Grant began casting around for a new approach. He decided to set his new book ten years ahead. That way, he said, there was more scope for invention. I had no idea he was going to handle it as he did. His judgment was clouded by his need to succeed, and the book is destructive on several levels, including the personal."

"You hold strong views on it," Claxby observed. "And what do you mean by the personal level?"

"I'm thinking of Lloyd Cooper. The description, intended or not, shouldn't have happened. And the whole ethos of the book, quite apart from that, worries me. It portrays a violent, lawless society. The so-called hero is an arsonist. In Grant's other books, harmless whodunits, there was always a high degree of optimism. I didn't mind participating in those. If the story line needed a laboratory background—scientific data, cryptograms, that sort of thing—I was happy to provide details. But for this book, *The Helius Factor*, I felt extreme distaste. My work became a chore. An unpleasant one."

"He was relying on you for his scientific data?" Claxby asked. "In what way are you qualified?"

"I'm a trained scientist. I studied for my degree at Columbia University."

Claxby, with an abrupt movement, got out of his chair and walked over to the window. He was frankly disbelieving. "You're telling us you threw over a scientific career in order to take on hack work for a writer of crime stories?"

"I got out for reasons of conscience," Dwight explained patiently. "I believed my research would be for the common good. It wasn't. I took on hack work, as you call it, because the book world appealed to me. It was refreshingly different, and perhaps more importantly, it gave me freedom."

Claxby looked at him thoughtfully for several moments before going back to his chair and sitting again. "Your conscience," he said at last, "fascinates me, but I'm even more interested in facts. You gave up your scientific work, so you tell us, because you disapproved of what you were asked to do. You then got this job with Grant. Eventually, you became uncomfortable even with that when Grant changed direction. But you kept on assisting him. You didn't quit. Why? Did you find some compensation, perhaps? An attractive and compelling reason for staying on?"

Dwight, aware of the allusion to Fay, forced himself to stay calm. "In time I might have persuaded Grant to modify his excesses. Had I left, he would have hired someone else to help him with the research side. I couldn't influence him with this book; I might have been more persuasive with the next one. Had there been a next one. Those are the arguments we use when we're getting rather too old for the grand gestures, I suppose. I'm not a young man anymore."

The image of the elderly Connors didn't cut any ice with either police officer; he was young and virile enough, after all, to attract a wealthy widow.

Claxby asked him what his future plans were. "You are now out of a job."

Dwight shrugged. "It's early yet. I haven't had time to think about it. There are up-and-coming young writers who might be glad of my expertise. I was talking to Scott Wilson in the bar yesterday evening after the presentation. Apparently one of the writers had told him of my supportive role. From what I can gather, Wilson's novel is to do with medical mayhem. It might be a lot of rubbish. I haven't seen it. He wanted my advice about getting background information on genetic engineering. He also wanted to know if there was any possibility of so-called sensitive material finding its way into print."

Claxby, suspecting that this was a diversion, ignored it and steered Connors back on course. "Why—and how—do you suppose Grant died?"

Dwight looked at him levelly. "I don't know. Obviously, whoever wrote that note bore him one hell of a grudge." He turned to Maybridge. "Your lecture was probably rather too thorough, chief inspector. A book is like a brain child. It may be cretinous. It may be puny. But it's an odd parent who doesn't love it."

"A macabre—and unnecessarily violent reaction—wouldn't you say?" Maybridge's voice was sharp as he held on to his temper.

Claxby drew the conversation around to Lady Grant again. "If Grant's widow inherits, she'll be a very rich woman."

Dwight agreed. "But he had a divorced first wife, Gina, and twin daughters of about fourteen. She must have a claim, too."

"The daughters are by his first wife?"

"Yes. He's educating them, of course, and giving their mother a large allowance, which is paid on condition she doesn't remarry during Grant's lifetime. According to the terms of the will, she also receives a substantial lump sum on his death."

"How is it he took you into his confidence on this?" Claxby looked surprised.

"He asked me to witness the will."

"So you also know how much Lady Grant will inherit?"

Dwight answered him sharply. "No, certainly not. I didn't read the will. And 'in confidence' was misleading. He spoke quite freely of his intentions. It was in character that he should look out for Gina and the children—and make sure they were well provided for in the event of his death. Gina isn't a career woman, and technically she was the innocent party in the divorce. He wouldn't shirk his responsibility. Of that I'm certain."

"But the largest part of the estate will, of course, go to his present wife, Lady Grant."

Dwight didn't answer.

"Will you stay on with her for a while? Give her your emotional support?" The question was suave but loaded with implication.

"She's an independent woman quite capable of walking on her own."

Until you walk with her and bed with her, Claxby wanted to say. He had hoped to provoke Connors into a garrulous defense of his relationship with Fay, but he was too guarded to put the comment into play.

"What I want from you now," he asked instead, "is a concise statement of what you did last night." He pointed to Constable Radwell, who was sitting in some confusion behind the desk, trying to sort out the essential information from the irrelevant. "The constable will take it down verbatim."

Dwight, with a strong sense of reprieve, complied. He had gone to bed just before midnight. Before retiring, he had turned the gas heater off. In the morning, it was switched on, so someone had been down in the night. He had fallen asleep quickly and hadn't awakened until Ulysses began yelling. His bedroom was around the corner from Grant's—too far away for him to hear anything. He didn't know that Grant had been found dead until Dr. Crofton had come into his bedroom and told him.

"Did he describe the mutilation?" Claxby asked.

"I went to Grant's room with Crofton and saw it. This was after Chief Inspector Maybridge had informed Lady Grant."

"You and the doctor were alone in the room with Grant's body?"

"Alone at the door for a couple of minutes."

Claxby's anger with Maybridge showed briefly, but he said nothing. Maybridge knew it was deserved. His concern with Fay had, to say the least, been unprofessional. It was impossible to lock Grant's door, but he should have stayed within view of it until it was sealed.

"We didn't go in," Connors said. "We didn't touch anything. Your clues should still be pristine and unsullied." He then asked Claxby if he had to sign the statement.

"Not yet. Official statements will be made later at the police station. We'll know more when the handwriting has been analyzed."

Dwight stood up. "Some of the authors have jobs to go to tomorrow. They're pestering me to know how long they're likely to be kept here."

"Then they'll have to pester you for a while longer. I can't tell you anything definite yet." Claxby dismissed him. "All right, Mr. Connors, thank you. That's all for now." He waited patiently for him to leave before turning to Maybridge. "I understand that you're under considerable stress. Even so . . ."

Maybridge acknowledged his negligence and apologized for it. "Unfortunately, the door had a bolt but no lock."

Claxby didn't pursue the matter; if someone had written that sort of note to him and taped it over a corpse, he might have wandered off in a state of rage and confusion, too.

Changing the subject, he asked Maybridge what he thought of Connors, his genius for prevarication notwithstanding.

Maybridge remembered that he had once mentioned cryptograms. "Where would he get trained in cryptology?"

"A scientific brain can invent anything. What else?"

"Scott Wilson seems to have spoken of his manuscript with a lot of enthusiasm—so why didn't he go back home and fetch it?" Maybridge had checked Wilson's address; he lived in furnished accommodation, in a house intended mainly for students and less than a ten-minute drive away.

But Claxby didn't think that was relevant, either. It was probably a lot easier to talk about a book than to produce one. Wilson might have left it at home deliberately—not finished, perhaps, or not as good as he'd hoped it would be. Besides, he was carrying on with Bonny Harper. Why bother with fiction when a girl with loose morals and nice legs took you to bed?

"As I see it," he said, "one of the simpler solutions will turn out to be right. Grant could have died naturally. We'll find out soon. The more difficult problem is the mutilation." He suggested that after they'd had something to eat, he should carry on with the interviews himself while Maybridge went down to headquarters to see what kind of progress was being made with the handwriting analysis. "After all," he pointed out, "the note was addressed to you. It's only right that you should deal with your own correspondence."

Chapter NINE

Maybridge drove out of the grounds of St. Quentin's feeling immense relief. It was good to get away from the place—and its atmosphere—for an hour or so. He and Claxby had had a late lunch of cold lamb and salad during which neither of them had spoken very much, and a heavy gloom had descended.

This time yesterday, Maybridge thought as he took the road along the downs, I was arriving. I had my box of slides showing puny little murders. My lecture didn't seem likely to cause any problems, and I was even looking forward to the fun I was going to have. He felt a sudden need for fresh air and rolled down the window.

The interview with Connors was, he believed, the most significant. His diatribe against Grant's book had seemed honest, and he had been determined to make his feelings known. Prevarication, as Claxby had suggested? Or did it go deeper than that? He had certainly manipulated the interview to a large extent. He was a complex man, capable of double standards and fond of exposing his conscience—an ambivalent conscience. Had he left Grant and taken Fay with him, the divorce settlement, if any, would have been small; Fay would have been the guilty party. Obviously, Grant had felt an obligation toward his first wife; he had probably divorced her for Fay. That he was paying her generous maintenance while

she remained unmarried implied that she hadn't left him for
another man.

In the case of Fay and Connors that wouldn't apply. The
financial motive had to be a strong one. For them Grant's
death was a financial asset—too convenient, surely, to be
natural. It was very convenient, too, that Grant was diabetic.
It would have been quite easy to switch an ampoule of insulin
for a stronger brand, or a different poison. Neither Fay nor
Connors had access to drugs. But Crofton was a surgeon and
had been in the room alone with Connors for a while. He'd
never live that procedural slip down any more than he'd live
down the bloody note! But why should the doctor assist
Connors in murdering Grant? Grant's death could be of no
possible advantage to him.

Maybridge braked as the lights turned red. The dirty ex-
haust of a heavy lorry waiting in front polluted the air, and
he was forced to close the window again, suddenly feeling
very tired and irritable. Grant had only been dead a few
hours, but it felt more like days. It was difficult to think it
through clearly, but he had to keep trying.

The previous evening at dinner, he remembered, Christopher Haydon had talked about drugs. He had suggested that
Grant might be on mindbenders. A sarcastic comment or a
considered observation? And who better than he to provide
them? As a pharmacist, he enjoyed even easier access than
Dr. Crofton and Kate Cooper. The box he had tried to hand
up to his father on the stage contained something incriminating, or even dangerous. The old man had been badly worried
by it. It was unfortunate he had looked so sick at that stage of
the interview. If he was in too fragile a state of health to be
forced to say what was inside, then Christopher would have
to be interviewed, and if necessary, bullied into a confession.
It was necessary to know.

The traffic began moving again, and he changed gears to
overtake the lorry.

Christopher had left for home during the night, but his father had been roaming the premises. He could have plunged in the skewer after going down to the car to check on Marcus. Grief could have built up into action. Denied, of course.

Another writer known to have been up during the night was Bonny Harper. But of all the authors interviewed, she had sounded the most honest, though he couldn't be absolutely sure of her, either. They were probably all lying like hell. He felt too personally involved, too persecuted, to be fair. *They* were the fiction experts, weren't they? They played with murder, orchestrated it like a symphony, wrote it up on their typewriters, and then taunted him with his inability to catch them. Someday in the future, he thought sourly, he might see the humor of it. He didn't now.

When he arrived at the police station, he went straight through to Inspector Barker's room. Barker was totally absorbed in the job at hand; that Maybridge was a prime target for amused comment didn't occur to him. "Good," he said briskly, "you've come. I was about to send for you." "Sir" was only added as an afterthought.

That Barker had attended one of the better public schools, followed by three years at Oxford, and had then opted for a career in the police force wasn't so unusual these days. His high-handed manner had nothing to do with his schooling or background. He always became extremely interested in whatever job was assigned to him and couldn't be bothered with the niceties of rank. Maybridge, as chief inspector, was one grade up and considerably his senior in age, hence the "sir." But mostly he forgot it.

"Good God," Maybridge said.

Pinned on a pegboard on the wall facing the window were photostats of thirty-one postcards inviting Maybridge to FAULT THIS MURDER, DETECTIVE CHIEF INSPECTOR MAYBRIDGE, IF YOU CAN. They were three times the original size and seemed to shout like a devil's chorus from the depths of hell. Under each, on neat little strips of paper, was typed the name of the writer.

"Well, there they are," Barker boomed proprietorially, as if he'd invented them. "The originals are being fingerprinted."

"Oh, Jesus," Maybridge whispered. He wondered if Rendcome, the chief constable, had seen them. One, small and neat, pinned over the corpse, had been shocking enough; thirty-one were mind-blowing.

"Here's a copy of the one written by the murderer, or the mutilator," Barker said, indicating one of similar size on his desk. "Enlarged to this size, it shows all the idiosyncrasies very clearly indeed. Take that one over there—top left. Notice how the capital F looks like the frayed end of a piece of cotton. It's symptomatic of heart disease. Normally, you'd need a magnifying glass to see it. Your murderer—well, whoever wrote the note—shows it to a lesser degree. In his case, it could be a mild illness—a fatigue, perhaps. Do you see what I mean?"

Maybridge's own heart, normally a hundred percent healthy, had gone into overdrive. He forced himself to be calm. Barker was pointing to a note written by someone called Elwyn Pringle, a writer he hadn't come across.

"Are you telling me he's the one?"

"Oh, no," said Barker, "quite the contrary. Look at the angle of the lines. Pringle's are arched. The murderer's ascend. He's self-assertive. Pringle isn't. One can't be too dogmatic about these things, but I'd say Pringle is sick."

"Who, then, out of the remaining thirty did it?"

But Barker refused to be rushed. "When you're dealing with majuscules and minuscules, it's easier. Here the letters are all majuscules." He noticed Maybridge's puzzlement and explained impatiently, "Capitals are called majuscules; the small letters are minuscules. The descenders of minuscules go into the lower zone. The majuscules don't, so that cuts out lower-zone analysis."

"I should be very grateful," Maybridge retorted sharply, "if you'd cut out the jargon and just tell me."

Barker had thick fair hair that fell across his forehead. He jerked his head from time to time in an impatient gesture. When he was excited or worried, he jerked it frequently. "The science of graphology requires time and care. There is no such thing as identical handwriting any more than finger-prints are identical. I have been working extremely hard on these samples; there must be no error."

"You mean you haven't finished?"

"Yes, I have. Just before you arrived, in fact."

"And the verdict?"

"You're not going to like this," Barker warned, "and I'm sorry if I disappoint you . . ."

For a crazy moment, Maybridge was convinced that Barker was going to implicate Fay. He forced the conviction from his mind. "Well, go on," he said impatiently. "Who?"

"Nobody," Barker said.

It occurred to Maybridge that an intelligent young officer who was undoubtedly brilliant in some directions could fall down sadly in others. "Much as I appreciate your ability," he told him, "you're not one of the acclaimed experts in the field."

"I would be," Barker snapped immodestly, "if my time wasn't taken up with police work."

That, Maybridge had to admit to himself, though not to Barker, could well be true. All the same, you didn't dismiss a whole wallful of suspects quite that easily.

He picked up the copy of the murder note from the desk and walked over to the suspects' notes. Doing so was as dis-tasteful as looking down the barrels of thirty-one guns, though these were paper missiles. They couldn't kill him, goddam them, just tear holes in his reputation.

He began with Lloyd Cooper's note. "This one——" he said to Barker. "Why not this one?"

Barker, rather huffily, came over and stood beside him. "His margins are wider, and so are the spaces between the lines. Cooper exaggerates; he's also given to vanity. His T bars are short, whereas they're long and strong on the murder note. Cooper isn't a leader. He's probably your typical writer—shuts himself away, introspective, but with a pretty high opinion of himself."

"And the man who wrote the murder note—a leader, you say?"

"Possibly a military type—likes to take charge. He can keep his feelings under control, but when he reaches flash point, watch out!"

Maybridge looked for the major's note. "Would you say Lawrence Haydon was a military man?"

"He could be, but not from choice. If pushed into battle, he wouldn't be happy about it. He wrote that note slowly and with a slight pressure. You can hardly see his T bars. The whole thing slopes backwards."

"What about Crofton?" The doctor, at least, had a dominant personality. Maybridge looked for his note.

"Written at speed," Barker said. "Impulsive, acquisitive. Can be exceedingly careful when necessary. Where some of the letters aren't properly formed, he's gone back over them. He's a local surgeon, isn't he?"

"Yes, a heart specialist. Writes books to make money for the hospital."

"How extraordinarily altruistic," Barker said. "You surprise me."

Trevor Martin's specimen was pinned next to the doctor's. "How would you analyze this?"

"Extreme discontent," Barker said briefly. "What sort of books does he write?"

"Murders, like the rest of them. He wrote a book based on the Haigh case but doesn't know his chemistry."

"If he wanted to dispose of a body," Barker said, "a living

body, not a fictional one, he'd make sure he knew what he was doing."

"Based on what you see in his handwriting?"

"Certainly."

Barker indicated the note written by Scott Wilson. "Here's your most complex character. Some of the capitals are so close they mingle. Of the lot on this board, probably the most interesting. Absolutely not the same writing as the murder note." But Maybridge could see that for himself.

Cora Larsbury's note was pinned above Wilson's. It was the small, typically neat handwriting that so many women of her age and education used. His own mother had a similar hand. "What would you say about Mrs. Larsbury?"

"Briefly, elderly. The spacing between the words is narrow. She's probably impatient, talkative, jealous, perhaps. Moody, certainly. But she isn't the mutilator; that's obvious. None of them is."

Maybridge didn't ask for a character analysis for all the notes, but he compared each one with the murder note before finally giving up.

"It seems you're right," he admitted at last.

"I'm not a fortune-teller in a fairground," Barker said, running his hand several times through his hair and then flicking it back. "What I've told you is just the cream off the milk—entertainment for the layman but nonetheless valid for that. Graphology is useful in psychological studies, but when those notes were handed to me, I wasn't asked to probe a mutilator's mind. I was asked to compare thirty-one copies to the original. I had to look for margins and slants, width and speed, angle of lines, pressure, simplicity, embellishment, and so on."

Maybridge lit a cigarette and inhaled deeply. "Was the murder note written by a man or a woman?"

Barker pushed over the lid of a tape container before answering. "Use that tin as an ashtray if you must smoke.

Man or woman—that's not as easy to answer as you might think. There are effeminate men—masculine women. In other words, all have some characteristics of the opposite sex."

"So we're not dealing with the aggressive male?"

"I didn't say that. I wish you wouldn't misinterpret me."

"Could it have been written by a homosexual?"

"Yes."

"So that narrows it?"

"No it does *not*. You want everything to be black and white."

"I want an arrest," Maybridge said mildly. "And the only person who attended my lecture and didn't copy that note is the son of a major who, according to you, would much rather have been something else. The son is a homosexual."

"It's the older generation who's always so censorious," Barker said impatiently. He added "sir" and again made it sound like an insult.

Maybridge, unruffled, asked if he might make a phone call. He had to contact Claxby.

Claxby received the news about Christopher Haydon with equanimity. Based on elimination, it was still quite probable nevertheless. He said he'd have him recalled. In the meantime, he told Maybridge, he'd been in touch with the pathologist. Grant's death had been due to hypoglycemia, as they'd originally thought, due to a massive overdose of insulin. It could have been self-administered, though that was extremely unlikely. Given the absence of any tangible suicide motive, you didn't pump yourself full of insulin because you'd had a row with a few people and your infant son had made an unwelcome appearance. It didn't make sense. And though the syringe and vial had Grant's fingerprints on them, it also had Lady Grant's.

"It's not unusual for the wife of a diabetic to handle the stuff," Claxby told Maybridge, "but as only those two prints

are on the syringe and vial, we can't let the little lady waltz
away into the arms of her lover without any further investigation. I suggest you get back here and take over the rest of
the interviews. When you arrive, I'll drive her to headquarters
so that she can make a full statement."

Maybridge felt as if a steel bar had been pushed down his
spine and then drawn out fast again. "Did you compare her
fingerprints with the one on the postcard?"

"You mean, with a faint and possibly smudged one? No,
that would have been no good. When she went down to
make the identification this morning, she volunteered to be
printed . . . Well, to be more precise, it was suggested that it
might be a good idea. There were so many prints in Grant's
bedroom, it helped to clarify things."

"I see," Maybridge said quietly, and he replaced the receiver.

Barker was looking at him keenly. "Progress?"

"Claxby thinks so." He turned around in his chair and
looked up at the notes again. "How would you analyze Dwight
Connors? The fourth from the left, middle row?"

Barker let out a heartfelt and pointed sigh before tackling
the question.

"Occasional irregularity in the spacing. High-placed T bars.
Letters taper toward the end of the word. Increasing left-hand
margins. Opportunist at times—an idealist, perhaps. Not con-
sistent. But what's that got to do with anything?"

Maybridge couldn't answer. He could have asked Barker to
analyze Fay's writing, but he didn't. It would be like asking
him to undress her in public. He was in no hurry to go back.
Claxby's tone of voice grated on him. He had been too quick
to assume Fay's guilt. And too pleased about it.

"I could do with coffee," he told Barker.

"Right, sir." This time there was no insolence in the "sir."

"Here or in the canteen?"

"Here." Maybridge didn't want to have to make conversation with anybody. He wished Barker would go out and leave him on his own, but Barker had no intention of doing anything of the kind. He had been hauled away at no notice from a language course that he had been attending with a holiday in Yugoslavia in mind. The holiday would be spent studying the architecture of the minarets and mosques, mainly in Bosnia and Macedonia. Later, for his own amusement, he would write a booklet on it. All his field studies, archaeological digs, and wanderings in the pursuit of knowledge were carefully written up afterward. He had never attended a writers' seminar. The idea interested him. Maybridge would tell him all about it.

Maybridge, sipping coffee and trying to compose himself, could think of better topics of conversation, if he had to talk at all. Nevertheless, he decided to humor Barker and remembered he had the program that Grant had given him. It was folded neatly in the inner pocket of his wallet and still contained Grant's letter urging him to attend. He removed it before passing the program across the desk to Barker. "Have a look for yourself."

While Barker scanned the program, Maybridge, for something to do, reread Grant's letter. He could almost hear Grant's richly self-assured voice speaking to him. We'd be delighted if you'd come along. A retired police officer from London was due to give a talk on ballistics, but he's been laid low by appendicitis. If you could fill the gap, we'd be more than grateful. It's a small club . . .'

The letter was written, not printed.

Even so . . .

An insane and completely impossible idea began forming in Maybridge's mind. He tried kicking it out but couldn't. Placing the letter on the desk, he asked Barker to analyze it. "It's from Grant."

Barker, absorbed in the program, looked up irritably. Then he looked at Grant's letter, and his irritation vanished.

"Good grief, how extraordinary!" He placed it next to the

murder note and flicked his hair back several times with ex-
citement. "By God, just look at it!" He touched the letter
gently, as if it were a rare and precious fragment of parch-
ment, and ran his fingers excitedly under the lines. "Not many
majuscules but enough to go on." He took out a magnifying
glass and peered through it. "The minuscules are formed like
majuscules here and there, and even if they weren't, the whole
thing is totally characteristic—the spacing, the pressure, the
slope." He shook his head in wonderment and began to smile.
"Well, there you are," he said to Maybridge. "There you *are*
without the single shadow of a doubt."

A stunned Maybridge wondered fleetingly where he was.
In a lunatic asylum, perhaps. He protested that the allegation
was bloody ridiculous. He refused to believe it. He had a
feeling he was being conned—not by Barker but by Grant's
cadaver now lying in the mortuary. Barker took him through
all the relevant capital letters and then started on the minuscules, showing how they were sufficiently characteristic to
prove his point. "Absolutely unmistakable," he said triumphantly. "We're home and dry! If I'd had this letter in the
beginning, I'd have been spared hours of work. Grant wrote
the murder note himself."

Maybridge pushed back his chair and walked over to the
notes on the wall, which now seemed to blend together into
one long howl of derision. He turned his back on them. His
heart was thumping too fast. He could do with a whiskey.
He could do with hitting somebody hard.

Chapter TEN

Maybridge took some slow deep breaths. "Why," he asked Barker, "should Grant take an overdose of insulin, write that note, pin it to his headboard, lie down on his bed and die, and later offer up his carotid artery to a skewer?"

Barker didn't know. Nor did he care. "That's your problem, sir."

And Claxby's, Maybridge suddenly remembered. How the hell was he going to explain this to the superintendent. He decided he needed professional backup. "You've persuaded me, against reason and judgment," he told Barker, "and now you've got to help me persuade the superintendent."

Barker met Maybridge's eye and this time knew better than to argue. "Very well"—he sighed—"if you insist."

During Maybridge's absence, Claxby had gotten through several interviews at considerable speed. The writers, for the most part, had spent all night in their rooms, asleep. A few admitted to going to the lavatory. They had all spoken well of Grant. He had been kind, brilliant, helpful, a good chap. The strongest adverse criticism leveled was that he had been tactless. And as for skewers, while admitting to knowing what a skewer looked like, the writers tended to speak of them with some reserve. "Useful for skewering meat, Superin-

tendent, on the few occasions when a working scribe could
afford a roast to skewer—but as for putting the implement to
any other use . . ." Here hands had been spread wide and
eyes rolled in appalled innocence. Claxby believed them.
Maybridge's phone call about Christopher Haydon had underlined his belief and put a full stop after it.

He sent for Lawrence Haydon and told him that he intended to phone his son to ask him to come back and copy
the note. "It's only right there should be no exceptions."

"But he's in London."

"Which isn't exactly the antipodes," Claxby pointed out.
"It won't take him long to return. Perhaps you'd like to phone
him yourself from here?" He pushed the phone toward him
across the desk.

They rang the number unsuccessfully several times; then
Maybridge came in with Barker. Claxby told Haydon to leave
it to him. "I'll call you if I get through." He had a mental
image of Christopher aiming his car in the direction of
Heathrow.

And later, listening to what Barker and Maybridge had
to tell him about the note, he tended to cling to the former
image. It was totally impossible to replace it with anything
based on the information he had just been given.

"Under different, less serious, circumstances," he told the
two officers, "I'd say you were pulling my leg." He turned
to Constable Radwell. "What's your opinion of it?"

Radwell wanted to laugh but didn't dare. "Quite unbelievable," he said, suitably solemn.

Barker was beginning to lose his temper. "Believable or
not, it's true."

Maybridge stood at the window, looking out at Lloyd and
Kate Cooper, who were walking together across the lawn.
It was easier to observe Lloyd now and see the man, not the
scars. That he was able to walk out there with his wife showed
a degree of emotional healing, due possibly to circumstances

a great deal more appalling than anything he'd encountered
so far. He was learning the hard way to get his disfigurement
into perspective. That they were both guilty in each other's
eyes was obvious, but that they could still walk together,
despite believing it, showed a depth of feeling that was good
to see.

Over on the croquet lawn, Bonny had removed the hoops
and was playing a form of bowls. She rolled the balls with
some viciousness, and most of them ended up in a small
circular rose bed. Scott Wilson retrieved them. Maybridge
wondered if the roses were Silver Ballerinas. At this distance,
he couldn't be sure. Ulysses, like a bored old man in a pixie
bonnet, sat in his pram, looking on. Maybridge suddenly
thought of Fay and wondered if Claxby had said anything
to her yet about making an official statement. Or was he leaving it to him to tell her? He ran a few reassuring phrases
through his mind to preparation. Just in case.

"All right," Claxby said to Barker at last, "I accept that
what you're telling me you're telling me in good faith, but I
want a second opinion. I'm not questioning your judgment
or trying to belittle you. I know you've had training in this,
but when the circumstances are bizarre, and you must admit
that they are, it seems sensible to have another expert in on
it." He looked over to Maybridge. "Wouldn't you agree?"

"I suppose so." Did it take two doctors to certify a lunatic?
he thought.

Claxby looked at him with extreme disfavor. "You've
landed us in this," he said bitterly. "You taunted them about
their books, and they retaliated by making you—and the rest
of us—a laughing stock. What am I supposed to tell the
press officer? What do I tell the chief constable? For heaven's
sake, you stand by that window admiring the view as if none
of this concerns you. You give me an unsolvable problem
that has overtones of paranoia, and you don't even try to
suggest a solution."

"That's because I haven't got one," Maybridge said quietly. He understood Claxby's ire and sympathized with it. He wished he could take early retirement and get the hell out of this place. He wished he had already taken it.

There was a knock on the door, and Brian Anderson came in.

"Not now," Claxby said brusquely.

"I've got to speak to you." Anderson was obviously agitated.

"*Not now*," Claxby repeated louder.

Nevertheless, Anderson closed the door behind him and advanced with determination. "It's about Christopher Haydon."

Claxby said, "Please, some other time." He wanted to shout, "*Go away!*" but restrained himself.

"His father told me you've been phoning his flat."

"Yes, and I'll be trying again soon." In these new circumstances, there might be no point in recalling him, but he still couldn't believe what he had been told. So the younger Haydon had better come back.

"He's not in London," Anderson said, fingering his hearing aid.

"Oh, isn't he?" Claxby asked. And presumably not taking flight from the nearest airport, either, if Barker's wild assertion was correct.

Anderson, like a gnarled old tree, stood rooted to the carpet. His face had a slightly yellow tinge, and his eyes were bloodshot. He looked at Claxby with despair.

"He's in his car—in the back parking ground."

"Oh?" said Claxby.

"In the trunk," Anderson said. His voice rustled like dead leaves. "He's been there all night."

Certain events tend to stay in the mind, strong in color and vivid in detail. The next half hour stayed with Maybridge like a dreaded recurring dream. Now, living it for the first time, he followed Anderson out of the room, through the hall, and out the front door. There was a small wind flicking through the bushes and scattering fallen chrysanthemum petals like drops of colored rain. The air smelled good, sweet as young apples. The old man stomped his way around the building, past the kitchen area, and into the cobbled stable yard that served as a parking area. The stables, flanked by two urns containing tired-looking geraniums, held four cars. Maybridge recognized Grant's maroon Bentley gleaming like a well-groomed beast in the shadowy interior. Next to it was a brown Mercedes, equally opulent. In the other stable was a jaunty TR6 with a crooked number plate, keeping company with a twenty-year-old Ford that seemed to brood over it like an elderly relative. A white Rover was parked on the far side of the stables, facing toward the cobbled yard. Dangling from the back window was a small toy rabbit held by a blue ribbon.

Anderson pointed to a window above what was possibly a storeroom that faced out on to the yard. "My bedroom," he said. Everyone waited for him to say something else, but he didn't.

"Well?" said Claxby.

"My bedroom overlooks the yard. I saw what happened. The stable light was on. That's the car," he said, pointing to the white Rover.

At this point, Maybridge's stomach began to churn. He looked at the sky and saw small flaking clouds flapping across the blue like seagulls' wings. He heard Claxby opening the boot and then his muttered exclamation. Maybridge lowered his eyes in a swift movement so that he was spared looking into the boot. Here on the cobbles was a small dark pool that at first glance could have been petrol but wasn't. He raised his eyes cautiously, his fists clenched in his pockets, and took several deep breaths.

The trunk wasn't very big, but neither was Christopher. He fitted comfortably, neatly, in fact, huddled in the fetal position, his head supported by his knees. His jersey, a clean bright yellow the previous day, was now streaked with brown. His hair was stiff with dried blood, and particles of broken skull showed through like a smashed seashell.

"A few years ago, Grant saved my engineering firm from bankruptcy," Anderson said. In the present context, it seemed the most irrelevant remark ever dropped into an abyss. All four officers looked at him with uncomprehending eyes.

"I was caught out on the stock market," Anderson went on.

He lost his audience as everyone concentrated on the corpse again.

Claxby pointed at the wing mirror. The sharp edges were coated with rusty-looking blood. "That could have done it— or started it. After that, a very frenzied attack. Look at the bruising at the back of the neck; you can almost see the finger marks."

"He was a man of considerable generosity," Anderson persisted, like a guest speaker at a dinner to whom no one wanted to listen. He couldn't hear what Claxby was saying but was quite determined that Claxby and the others should hear him out. He raised his voice several decibels. "It takes a long time to know a person. Outwardly, Grant appeared unsympathetic, but when it came to the crunch, he was there. I'm forever in his debt. I'm not a man to forget old friendships. Loyalty to me is the supreme virtue."

"What do you suppose he's on about?" Claxby asked Maybridge irritably.

Maybridge spoke thickly through the bile rising at the back of his throat. "I think he's trying to tell us that Grant did this." He gestured at the corpse. There was congealed blood on all exposed areas of skin; it must have spurted out like a fountain. Unlike Grant himself, Christopher, when attacked, had been very much alive.

Claxby turned his attention to Anderson. "What are you trying to say?"

"What?"

He spoke louder. "You're trying to tell me something. I'm listening."

For Anderson it was like a fighter plane crashing through the sound barrier. He boomed out his defense of Grant. "He arranged this seminar in the hope we'd all enjoy ourselves, and for his pain he was attacked from all quarters. That loose and dreadful woman brought her child. Lloyd Cooper made a disgusting exhibition of himself. Sir Godfrey's wife and his secretary flaunted their liaison. Lawrence Haydon should have crawled and apologized for plagiarizing his book instead of moaning like a martyr. And then, finally, Haydon—drunk and incapable—kills his own dog and blames Grant for it."

As a list of minor wounds, it was fairly impressive, but what, Maybridge wondered, had been the final catalyst?

"Are you trying to tell me that Grant murdered Christopher Haydon?" Claxby shouted the question.

"Clear and slow but not loud," Anderson advised.

It sounded like the score of a death dance, but Claxby got the meaning. He asked the question again.

Anderson heard it. "There was no malice aforethought. Had Grant lived, the verdict would have been manslaughter with mitigating circumstances." He pointed to the window again. "I saw it. I would have given evidence on his behalf."

Claxby, enunciating very clearly, asked him to describe exactly what he had seen.

Now that he had the full attention of his audience, Anderson went into some detail. "I was going to bed up there —in that room with the window overlooking this courtyard. Lady Grant was in charge of allocating the bedrooms, and she gave me the worst. It's small and stuffy, and the bathroom is down one flight of stairs. I don't like confined spaces. I'm not claustrophobic, but I can't stand a room that's too small. The only way to make the room bigger was to open the window, though that lets in the draft, of course. My feet were cold. I got out of bed to put my socks on, and I looked out through the open window, wondering whether I should close it or not. The yard light was on—another annoyance; it shone into my room.

"I saw Christopher Haydon walking over to his car. He unlocked it and got in. It wouldn't start. Then I saw Sir Godfrey walking over from the house toward his own car— that maroon Bentley over there. He saw Haydon having trouble starting the engine, and he turned away from the Bentley and went over to him, probably to see if he could help. That's the sort of man he was.

"Haydon then got out. He had something in his hand. Perhaps something to strike Sir Godfrey with. They were at the far side of the car, and I couldn't see clearly. The next thing I saw was Sir Godfrey taking a few steps back and Christopher Haydon seeming to thrust something at his chest. And then Sir Godfrey's patience snapped. He was like a boxer teaching a little whippersnapper a lesson. I don't think he meant to go as far as he did. He couldn't help himself. He took Christopher Haydon by the throat and began shaking him. Haydon kicked him in the groin, and then Sir Godfrey lost all control. He struck Haydon's head on the side of the car—on that mirror, I think—then picked him up and battered him against the car again. Finally, he let go, and Haydon sagged on the ground."

Anderson's normally pale face flushed red with distress. Deeply disturbed by the recollection, he carried on haltingly. "Sir Godfrey went and opened the trunk of the Rover, then came back and picked up the body and put it in—as you see it now. He stood looking at the car for two or three minutes. And then he went down on his knees and looked under it. I think he found the weapon—or whatever it was he was looking for—and he flung it over there by those bushes. It's up to you to find it." He paused and then, sensing he was about to be questioned, flapped his hands to quell the incipient jumble of sound. "No, no—you listen to me. I haven't finished.

I'll keep on telling you the answers to what I think you want to ask me. That way it's easier for all of us."

Maybridge and Claxby had never been silenced so effectively before. Anderson had a captive audience.

"I didn't know what to do. I sat on the side of the bed and thought about it. It would have been an act of friendship, I suppose, to have gone to Sir Godfrey to tell him that he had my full support. On the other hand, he must have been in a dreadful state of mind—confused, remorseful, worried. At a time like that, you need to be on your own. I thought, too, that he might have gone to you, chief inspector. You were on the premises. I didn't want to interfere. It didn't occur to me that he would go through the usual routine of injecting himself with insulin. I'd forgotten he needed it. This morning, when everyone talked about his being poisoned, I knew they were talking nonsense. He was too strong and brave a man to commit suicide, even though he might have thought he had good reason. I think he probably took too much insulin because he was in a state of shock and didn't know what he was doing. That bitch wife of his, if she had any feeling for him, should have looked in on him to see if he was all right. He was a lonely man. Had I gone down and spoken to him, he might have lived."

Anderson looked at his audience like a penitent before a row of priests. "My conscience," he said, "troubles me."

He went on before anyone could comment. "When I heard about the mutilation, I was horrified. I thought perhaps Lawrence Haydon had found out about his son's death and had taken revenge in that ghastly way. But when I was calmer, I couldn't believe it. Lawrence Haydon might whine about the plagiarism accusation, but he wouldn't take any other sort of action. Resigning from the Golden Guillotine Club was about his measure. He's a pathetic little man. Had he known about his son, he would have run weeping to the police. When it dawned on me that I was the only one who

knew about his son's death, I didn't know what to do. I knew
what I *should* do." He spoke directly to Claxby. "I should
have told you. There's a saying about speaking well of the
dead; I've always believed it. I think I tried to pave the way
by telling you all the good and positive things about Sir
Godfrey before divulging the one awful thing that had to be
divulged. I expected you to find the body at any moment. I
didn't realize it was going to take so long. It was when you
began asking his father about him that I knew I had to speak.
I was afraid his father might come out with you and see the
body before you could do something to make it look less
terrible. You had to be told. Even so," he added accusingly,
"you had to be forced to listen."

He looked at his hands. "You'll fingerprint the car, of
course. You'll fingerprint Sir Godfrey. And if you know your
job properly, you'll fingerprint me. I could have done it and
put the blame on Sir Godfrey. If this was one of my thrillers,
I'd probably write it that way. But it isn't. And I've told you
the truth. And I'm more sad about this than you'll ever know.
A good, very much maligned man committed one act of
violence—after great provocation. Don't condemn him."

As a speech in mitigation, Maybridge thought, it wasn't
bad. He had no doubt at all in his mind that it was true.
Grant, wild with fury, had murdered Christopher Haydon
and then, shocked and remorseful, had committed suicide. But
why, in God's name, had he penned that taunting note and
taped it to the headboard before overdosing himself? Any
man as distraught as that would have jabbed in the injection
and then crept into bed to die in total misery.

He looked back at the corpse with slightly less caution now
that he was getting used to it. Just what, he wondered, had
Christopher said to send Grant over the top like that? For
Grant to have battered him like a rag doll.

Claxby was speaking clearly and slowly to Anderson, in-
forming him that he had to make a statement.

"Of course," Anderson said irritably, "of course. Lead on—no point in wasting more time." He moved off across the yard.

Claxby, not yet ready, told Barker to accompany Anderson. "I'll be with you in a minute." He turned to Maybridge. "A weapon? Do you think that's likely?"

Maybridge was remembering the small gray box of the previous evening. Dueling pistols, Lawrence had joked bitterly, a Luger or a small incendiary. "It shouldn't take long to find out."

They started searching among the clump of hydrangea bushes that grew thickly along one corner of the wall, dividing the yard from the kitchen garden. Some small debris from the yard had blown into it. There were several sweet papers, a half-empty bag of crisps, an old torn handkerchief, and something that looked like a child's toy, only wasn't.

Radwell found it. The gray box had landed in two separate halves near it, and the little golden object was resting on several thin twigs near the base of the bush.

"Mock not," Maybridge said softly, "that ye be not murdered." He guessed that Christopher Haydon had made it himself. He doubted if the major, with his rather arthritic hands, would have had the patience or dexterity.

"But what is it?" Claxby, carefully holding back the hydrangea leaves, peered down at it.

"It's a guillotine," Maybridge said, "fashioned out of plywood and painted gold. The figure under the blade is made with pipe cleaners, the blood on the neck is a blob of sealing wax, and the white hair is cotton wool."

"You mean that Grant was handed an effigy of himself and killed because of it?" Claxby's voice was shrill with astonishment.

"I'm afraid so," Maybridge said. "The so-called final straw was a very lethal instrument."

Chapter **ELEVEN**

It is impossible to keep the news of two corpses, one murdered and one mutilated, from the reading public for more than a day. It is also impossible to incarcerate thirty crime writers in a university building normally used for student occupation. The students needed to get in. And the crime writers, for various reasons, needed to get out. Rendcome, the chief constable, went to St. Quentin's to assess the situation and to decide what had better be done. The press officer would need the guile of a politician to handle this one, but Rendcome told him to do his best. "Keep it short. Divulge nothing other than that it was sudden. And don't link Grant with Christopher Haydon yet. Tell them there'll be a full press conference tomorrow. We should know more by then."

When one corpse has been murdered by another, it cuts out the expense of a trial, which was one small plus. But there were so many minuses in this case that the equation refused to balance. Grant's death note taunting Maybridge—and the mutilation—were the two remaining puzzles that no one seemed able to solve. Grant, without doubt, had written the note. Grant, without doubt, had murdered Haydon. And Grant had sufficient knowledge of forensic science to know that he wasn't presenting Detective Chief Inspector Maybridge with an unsolvable mystery, so why taunt him with it?

Under the circumstances, why think of Maybridge at all. What sort of vitriolic lecture had the normally responsible Maybridge delivered to merit that sort of insane reprisal? Rendcome asked him and listened to the answer with some disbelief. "As from now," he warned him, "you'll avoid all literary get-togethers like the plague."

The censure, on the whole, was mild. It could have been much worse.

Claxby was still simmering. He'd had a day of it and felt tired. He wished the mutilation charge could be quietly filed away and forgotten, but of course that was out of the question. He had all the names and addresses of the suspects. He had their fingerprints on the postcards. As yet, no print could be clearly linked with the skewer. There were several smudged prints on Grant's murder note, though most of them were his own. Rendcome told him that the major issue was the two deaths and that they should be handled routinely to the best of everyone's ability. The mutilating presented more problems and might take more time. It was a pity, he added dryly, that Sir Godfrey couldn't have the kind of funeral that he would have had under different circumstances. Grant liked glory; Rendcome had known him rather well.

Claxby told Maybridge to call the writers together and tell them that they could pack their bags and go. "But stress that they might be recalled at any time." Claxby was taking Lady Grant down to the police station so that she could make her statement. He was now quite sure that she had had nothing to do with her husband's overdose, but even so, the statement had to be made. She had taken the news of Haydon's death, and the fact that her husband had caused it, with steely calm but had been deeply distressed by the major's reaction. The old man had wept, and Lady Grant had taken him in her arms. At that point, Claxby warmed to her a little, though Brian Anderson, quite plainly, hadn't. His antagonism, as he

watched her comforting the major, twisted up his features
into sour lines of disapproval. The prospect of driving the
three of them in the police car didn't give Claxby any pleasure,
but statements had to be taken from all of them, and Lawrence
Haydon had to make a positive identification.

Maybridge managed to see Fay before she left with Claxby.
The meeting was fortuitous. She was in the kitchen, giving the
staff their wages, when he happened to be passing. He paused
at the door, and she noticed him and suggested a quick coffee.

"If I have the time," she added. "Your superintendent was
born to his job. He left the womb clutching handcuffs. Dare
I keep him waiting?"

Maybridge smiled. "I accept responsibility."

They fetched two cups of coffee and sat drinking in silence.
He wanted to tell her how sorry he was that she had to suffer
the additional burden of the knowledge of Grant's guilt, but
he didn't know how to put it without making her obvious
pain even more unbearable by vocalizing it. She wanted to tell
him that his sympathy and his support were helping her
more than he could know, that she liked him as a person but
that, in the nature of things, they weren't likely to see each
other again.

He passed her the sugar. "Your seminar coffee is better than
the stuff they'll give you at the police station."

"If I'm offered any, I'll ask for tea."

"That's marginally worse."

She sipped her coffee, watching him over the rim of the
cup, her eyes troubled. "How can Lawrence Haydon be
helped?"

"No way that I know of."

"It's been pretty bloody."

"Yes, in every sense." He offered her a cigarette. She declined, though he lit one and inhaled deeply.

She asked him when his wife was returning from America.

"Soon, but not soon enough."

"She's a lucky woman."

"The luck's on my side."

Fay knew he meant it. She finished her coffee and stood up. He walked over to the door with her and saw Dwight Connors waiting by the lecture room. He guessed that they would want to talk privately before she left with Claxby.

She said, "I'd better go."

"Yes."

He held his hand out in an old-fashioned gesture. Slightly surprised by the courtesy, she extended hers, and they shook hands very formally.

"Thanks for everything," she said, "and I'm sorry for everything." That more or less summed it up.

Connors had asked the writers to assemble in the lecture room so that Maybridge could address them for the third and last time. He noted that Dr. Crofton had returned. The hospital emergency, if it had ever existed, was presumably over.

He told them that Grant's death had been caused by severe hypoglycemia following an overdose of insulin, probably self-administered. He said that Christopher Haydon had been found dead but didn't say where; nor did he comment on the manner of his dying. He guessed they knew, anyway. He told them they might be called upon to help the police with their inquiries at some later date. "And so," he said, "that's it."

"Not quite," Dr. Crofton boomed from the back of the room. "What about that nasty little piece of bloodless surgery with the skewer?"

Perhaps you are responsible for that, Maybridge thought. Who better qualified? It had probably taken some skill to find the carotid artery—a working knowledge of anatomy. He said the police were still investigating it.

But Dr. Crofton pressed on cheerfully. "Shame on you. Muriel Slocombe would have solved that in ten minutes flat. But that's by the by, I suppose. While I'm here, may I come up on the stage and remove my dust jacket?"

"By all means," Maybridge said.

Crofton's request had jogged his memory; other tedious details needed tidying up. Maybridge remembered that there were manuscripts in the office and that he had locked the door. "Those of you who have pieces of work to collect, come with me now."

Five of the novice writers found their literary offerings and departed. The sixth didn't. He was small and stout with basset-hound eyes and a neatly trimmed gray beard. He was an accountant by profession, he told Maybridge, as if this balanced the lunacy of writing books.

"My name is Pringle," the man with the beard continued, seemingly unperturbed by Maybridge's lack of response. "It's written on the cardboard folder containing the manuscript."

"Oh, yes?" said Maybridge, looking at him with slightly more interest. Barker had done an analysis on Pringle's handwriting. Not self-assertive and perhaps suffering from a mild illness had been his verdict. Something to do with the way he wrote the letter F.

Pringle hadn't looked sick a few minutes ago, but he was looking very troubled now. He explained that he had sent his manuscript to Grant a week ago and that Grant had said that he wanted to discuss it with him when he had time and that he had it in his office. "But it isn't here."

"Ask Dwight Connors about it," Maybridge suggested impatiently. "He handles the secretarial side. As far as I know, he's still in the lecture room."

"My manuscript is my life line," Pringle said despairingly. "It has been my one purpose in life for the last six months. I couldn't bear to lose it."

Maybridge suddenly thought of Christopher's battered body

with its daffodil-yellow jersey stained with blood and of Grant's handsome throat deftly pierced.

"Tough," he said without sympathy.

"You don't understand." Pringle's tone was accusing.

"Oh, but I'm sure Connors will. And now, if you'll excuse me, I've other things to do." Such as packing my pajamas, he thought. He opened the door, and Pringle, like a basset hound unjustly kicked, slunk out.

Upstairs, Maybridge looked around the small bedroom, feeling glad that he wouldn't have to spend another night in it. He was leaving St. Quentin's with a deep sense of defeat, the puzzle only half solved. He wasn't unduly ambitious, but he hadn't imagined that his promotion prospects would have been ended so abruptly. Skewered, in fact, like Grant's throat.

His head was muzzy, and he felt in need of fresh air. Dusk was falling, but he decided to take a last walk around the grounds. At the front of the building, Maybridge saw Kate Cooper sitting in the driver's seat of her Austin Cambridge while Lloyd and Scott Wilson loaded the trunk with Ulysses' folding pram and other baby paraphernalia. Bonny handed the infant over to Lloyd to hold. Ulysses, obviously not bothered about Lloyd's scars, beat a fat baby-fisted tattoo on his ear while his mother and Scott gave each other a long, tongue-probing kiss. A farewell, Maybridge wondered, or a prelude?

Trevor Martin was the next to leave. He owned an elderly but still very impressive Porsche. Probably bought second-hand, Maybridge thought; his teaching salary couldn't possibly stretch to a new one. He drove jerkily, gunning the accelerator in short stabs, clearly impatient to be gone.

Dr. Crofton drove a rusting two-seater that enclosed his large frame with only inches to spare. If the floor fell through, he'd wrap it around himself like a metal overcoat and walk it home. He noticed Maybridge standing on the grass verge and raised his hand in mock salute.

Maybridge nodded curtly. He stayed around until nearly all the cars, driven by their murder-orientated owners, had gone. It was like opening the gates of Parkhurst, he thought crossly, and ushering the inmates out.

In contrast to his mood, the evening was very pleasant. The air was bittersweet with the smell of flowers and of something burning. Little tendrils of gray smoke curled across the darkening sky, and Maybridge, curious as to the source of the fire, went to see who, if anybody, was in charge of it. A door from the stable yard led through to the kitchen garden, which was well tended, and a portable incinerator stood on a concrete slab, stuffed with paper.

Cora Larsbury, pitchfork in hand, was gently lifting the top layers so that the fire underneath had air. Flames leaped, died down, and leaped again. Scraps of scorched paper, light as butterflies, winged gently through the air. Cora moved backward from the incinerator when the flames became too menacing and cautiously fed the incinerator with more paper when they threatened to die. Like a pagan worshiper, she was totally absorbed; Maybridge found the scene fascinating and stood watching in silence. Cora, turning around to get fresh fodder from a canvas holder on the path noticed him. Her eyes were bloodshot with smoke, and her hands were streaked with grime. She was dressed in a pink jumper and skirt, thick gray stockings, and heavy shoes. She had wiped her hands on her skirt and soiled it. She looked like a wild and happy old lady playing dangerously with an uncontrollable element.

She smiled at him. "Good evening, chief inspector."

He returned her greeting and walked right into the garden. The gate behind him closed with a clunk. Over the wall he could hear the revving of car engines as the forensic squad took the murder car away. And then he heard nothing but the crackle of paper, the occasional whoosh of flame, and the sharp ping as Cora's fork struck the side of the incinerator.

"Lovely, isn't it?" she enthused.

"Yes, but have a care."

"Agni—Agni—Agni," Cora chanted softly. "Surya—Surya—Surya."

Maybridge didn't know anything about the Vedic Aryans and their worship of the nature deities. Cora knew very little, but she had heard of the mantras and liked the words. She translated for his benefit. "Agni is fire; Surya is sun. Hinduism, you know. The Veda is the sacred lore. I used it as background for a book on Indian."

"Published?" Maybridge asked unwisely.

Her eyes narrowed, but she didn't answer.

The sun had disappeared, and the moon lay hidden behind clouds, but the flames lit up the garden in a soft orange glow. Cora leaned on the garden fork, looking into the heart of the fire, and then began to sway from side to side as if in a ritual dance. "Agni—Agni—Agni—"

Maybridge remembered her words of the previous evening about her nonexistence and the flat lands of boredom. A manic-depressive? he wondered. Her swings of mood were extreme. Barker had summed her up very well—as he had summed up Pringle.

He wondered whose manuscript she was burning.

He told her about Pringle's loss. "He was very upset about it."

"Oh, dear." Cora smiled perversely. She went to the canvas holder, took out a sheaf of manuscript pages, placed the bundle on the pitchfork, and threw it on to the incinerator. Under the weight of it, the flames spluttered, then took hold of the edges and roared up redly, scattering ash.

Maybridge knew he had to move carefully. Speaking quietly, he asked how long it took to write a book.

"Oh, ages, chief inspector. You write it in your head—when you shop, when you drive, when you garden, when you bathe. And then you write it down." She moved nearer the flames and encouraged them by lifting some of the layers with the pitchfork. "My novel took me nearly a year."

"Is that so?" Maybridge said. "Is that a book you're burning now?"

Her eyes gleamed in the firelight. "Just rubbish, chief inspector. Nothing of any consequence."

"It looks like a manuscript," he persisted.

"It won't be in a minute," she said. "It's burning beautifully."

"Pringle," Maybridge told her, "called his manuscript his lifeline."

"We use many similes." She controlled her smile by biting on it.

"He also said it was his one purpose in life."

"Dear me, you had quite a talk."

"He said he had given it to Grant and that Grant had intended speaking to him about it."

"The past tense saddens me," Cora said without sadness.

Maybridge went to sit on the edge of a wheelbarrow loaded with chopped-up timber, which wasn't placed too near the incinerator. His mouth tasted bitter with smoke, and his eyes smarted.

He hadn't any patience with Pringle, but it was rather rough on him to have his book burned. Seated where he was now, he could see into the canvas holdall. The manuscript that Cora was burning had been typed on pale cream paper. The last forkful had gotten rid of the final chapter. Now exposed was the page of another manuscript on white paper. The leaping flames were as good as torchlight, and he could see the title, *Death in the Desert*, and typed underneath it: By Cora Larsbury. And scrawled across the side of the page in Grant's bold handwriting he read, "My dear Cora, why bother? You couldn't kill a captive fly with a sledgehammer, let alone write a salable murder mystery." There was more. Maybridge put his weight on his right leg and maneuvered himself into a better position so that he could read on.

"I would prefer you not to," Cora said quietly, "if you don't mind."

He almost overbalanced, and the wheelbarrow rocked at an alarming angle before righting itself. She had approached him silently, pitchfork in hand. With her white frizzed hair and wrinkled cheeks, she had the face of a reproving grandmother, but he sensed the menace of a strong and twisted will. She no longer seemed euphoric.

"I beg your pardon," he apologized.

"Comments like those," she said bitterly, "aren't easy to forget."

"I've already forgotten them," he lied gallantly.

She stood looking down at him. He eyed her warily. The pitchfork was formidable, and he knew he would be safer standing.

Once he had been held against a wall with a .38 revolver jabbing his ribs. He had managed to talk his way out of it. It made sense not to get into vulnerable situations. He stood up and suggested she might like to sit.

"Give me the fork. I'll prod the fire for you, keep it going."

She was reluctant to relinquish her weapon, but he stood smiling at her patiently and waited until she did. He helped the flames make an end of Pringle's manuscript, then thrust the fork into the soil behind the incinerator and returned to her. "It's all gone."

"Good," she said.

The smoke had cleared a little, and Maybridge felt the need for a cigarette. He took one out of the pack and lit it with a match. His lighter was out of fuel. "I'll have one, too," she said.

He lit it for her. She had chubby little hands with uncared-for nails and held the cigarette with the tip of her first finger and thumb as if she were holding a pen. She hadn't, he guessed, smoked for a long time. She didn't seem to like it very much. It was a prop.

"I can take constructive criticism," she said at last, "but not that sort. It shocked me."

"Pretty brutal," Maybridge agreed. "The mockery of a puny mind."

She looked at him sharply. "You don't have to humor me, chief inspector."

He told her that it was a considered comment. The lie came suavely, even though he wasn't quite sure how to handle her; you didn't tramp across ice with hobnailed boots. He suggested that she might like to tell him about it. "You mean, tell you about Pringle's manuscript?"

If that was the way she wanted to tell it . . . "Yes."

She drew on her cigarette with some distaste. "He and I became novice writers at about the same time. He didn't produce anything particularly brilliant. But this time, according to Sir Godfrey, his effort was pretty good. He mentioned it to a group of us when we were admiring the dust jackets on the stage. Next year, he said, Pringle's book could well be published and short-listed for the award."

She looked at the dying fire. It caught a few twigs at the base of the incinerator and sparkled up, crackling and dancing.

"I was curious to read it, but the only way I could get hold of his manuscript—and mine—was to fetch them from Sir Godfrey's office when everyone was in bed. The first time I attempted to get them, I had to go back to my room; Sir Godfrey and the Haydons were quarreling in the hall. I waited an hour and then tried again. This time there was no one around."

Maybridge asked how long she had taken to read the manuscript.

"Oh, I didn't read it right through, chief inspector; just enough to know it didn't deserve half the praise lavished on it—"beautifully observed, acutely perceptive, excellently plotted," and so on. And to make the contrast with mine even more obvious was the way he wrote his remarks. Pringle can't see very well—he has a cataract—so everything was very neatly printed. On my manuscript the comments were scribbled—well, you saw them—as if they weren't even worth the trouble of proper handwriting."

She removed a strand of tobacco from the side of her mouth, twisting her lips in distaste. "In my opinion, he overpraised a very ordinary novel written by a man without much writing talent but very skilled in financial matters. His accountant, in fact. Pringle handled Grant's business affairs and probably helped him to fiddle his income tax. You make my money grow and I'll get your book published—that sort of arrangement."

Maybridge tactfully said that it was likely.

"What annoyed me most," Cora confessed, "was the note he'd clipped to the title page. He'd printed it in large letters so that Pringle could read it easily before handing it over to you. He wanted you to read the book and then fault the murder if you could." She smiled at him slyly. "You and Superintendent Claxby have been very *slow*."

Maybridge ruefully agreed. Then he asked her what happened next.

She flushed. "I couldn't forgive the very derogatory—very unkind—comment about my not being able to kill. I saw it as a challenge."

"And your response to the challenge?' 'Maybridge probed.

She described it graphically—rubber gloves from the kitchen drawer, a skewer because it was easy to use, Grant conveniently lying on his back. "But the most dreadful irony of it all," she complained, "was that he was already dead."

"Insulin," Maybridge told her. "Probably self-administered."

"The bastard!" Cora replied.

Very sweetly, in the distance, a church bell began to ring.

This was Sunday evening, Maybridge remembered. People were going to church. Organs made quiet music: Old ladies prayed.

"After piercing him with the skewer," Cora said, "I pinned that note over the corpse." She dropped her unfinished cigarette and stood up. "That's about it," she said. "You asked me. Now you know."

Maybridge thanked her for telling him. "You'll have to tell the superintendent, too. He'll need an official statement."

"Oh, yes," Cora agreed. "I understand the procedure. But I foxed you all for a bit, didn't I. You'll credit me with *some* intelligence now, won't you?"

Maybridge assured her that she had foxed them very cleverly indeed. "You must try putting it in a book sometime," he added wryly.

"You are a kind man," she said almost wistfully. "You know I wouldn't hurt you."

Maybridge went over to see that the fire was safe and not likely to flare up and ignite St. Quentin's; not that he had any love for the place. When he went back to her, she was brushing down her skirt with grimy hands and making it worse. He offered to carry her holdall. She declined. Her manuscript, precious beyond price was in it; she would carry it herself.

He asked her, as casually as he could, if she had ever been in hospital. She told him she had had her hip joint done a while ago. But that wasn't the kind of hospital he had in mind.

It was quite dark now, and she took his arm in case she tripped as they walked out of the kitchen garden and around the building to the front parking ground. She had to go inside to fetch her coat and suitcase, and he said he would go with her.

"There's really no need, chief inspector. I won't run away."

"I wasn't thinking that for a minute," he lied, "but there might not be anyone on the premises now—lights might have been turned off. You don't want to fall, and I can help you with your suitcase."

She had done most of her packing, but there were still a few personal items on the dressing table. Maybridge noticed a photograph of a teenaged boy and a girl of about ten. They both had dark curly hair and posed with wide enthusiastic smiles. Cora said they were her grandchildren and spoke of them with pride. For the first time, Maybridge felt sorry for her—and for them.

"Nice youngsters," he said.

He carried her suitcase downstairs, and she followed him with the holdall. There were two cars left in the drive, an opulent Mercedes and a hatchback. Cora went over to the Mercedes and unlocked it. "You may drive it if you like," she offered. "I don't mind."

"This is yours?" He had been making for the hatchback.

"My husband doesn't allow me to use the Rolls," she complained. "In many ways, he's a mean man."

He looked at her in astonishment. "You own a Mercedes and a Rolls and you still want to write a *book*?"

She replied with dignity. "I've written several books, inspector. None of them published. I'd trade in my Mercedes, my Rolls, everything I've got, to see my books in print." She noticed his look of mystification and added, as Pringle had earlier, "But you wouldn't understand."

Epilogue

Five months after the seminar, Maybridge went on holiday with Meg to the Julian Alps. The choice of resort had been Meg's, influenced by Barker's most recently printed booklet on Yugoslavia. That Barker and his booklet tended to remind Maybridge of the seminar that he was trying hard to forget was unfortunate, but it couldn't be helped. Meg was a keen skier and hadn't been to that region before. She wanted to go. Later on, she had promised Maybridge, toward the end of the summer, they would go and lie on a flat, hot, boring beach and do nothing but soak up the sun.

To Maybridge, being bored was infinitely better than courting death on the slopes. He didn't ski and had no desire to try. While Meg was out, he spent his time in the hotel reading or taking walks on the safe areas of hard-packed snow. He had brought binoculars but didn't use them. Meg's bright red skiing jacket was ubiquitous; lunatics up there on the mountain wearing bright red skiing jackets were taking appalling risks. If one of them was his wife, he didn't want to know.

Meg, sensing this, was reluctant to tell him about the accident, but he had to be informed before someone else told him. She chose her moment when he was mellow, after a good dinner washed down by the almond-flavored Karlovački Bermet.

"This morning, one of the skiers had a mishap," she said. "Well, to put it bluntly, she died."

"Oh, Christ!" He put his hand over hers, quite roughly, with sudden fear. Why the *hell* had they come.

She moved her fingers under his grip and smiled. "Look," she said, "I'm here. You don't have to squeeze so tightly. It didn't happen to me."

"It's a crazy pastime."

"Not if you're careful."

"You're pushing fifty."

"What has that to do with it? This woman—"

"I don't care about any woman. If she wants to get herself killed, that's up to her. I care about *you*."

Meg persisted. "You might know this woman. I was standing with my ski group when her body was brought down. Some of the other skiers knew her—and her husband. She was once married to Sir Godfrey Grant."

Maybridge removed his hand slowly. Despite the warmth of the hotel dining room, he felt cold. Shock obliterated all sounds. The world out there and the world in here were white and silent and made of ice. He hadn't seen Fay since the seminar. He hadn't thought about her very much. He could have attended Grant's funeral, but there didn't seem any point in it. They weren't looking for Grant's killer. He had killed himself while in a state of shock after murdering Haydon. There had been no reason to think otherwise. And if there had been, there was still no proof; nothing to go on.

And so Connors had done it and scooped the pool, and now the bastard had killed Fay.

He wasn't aware that rage and mottled his features or that his forehead was wet with sweat.

Meg looked at him curiously. She hadn't meant to mislead him. He was thinking of the other one. "It's the first Mrs. Grant," she said, "the one he was married to before he was

knighted. They were divorced. She's now Mrs. Martin. She
married one of the writers shortly after her husband died."

It was impossible to hide his relief. The room was normal
again, filled with light and warmth.

Meg nodded as if confirming something to herself. She had
been right. He had liked the woman. Very much. But it wasn't
important; his love was for her.

"I think her name was Gina. Did you know her?"

Maybridge, still a compulsive smoker, took out his cigarettes
and lit one hungrily. "No."

He tried to recall what Connors had said about her. She
was the mother of Grant's twin daughters—young teenagers.
Grant was giving her a generous allowance, and she was to
inherit a substantial sum—had he said substantial?—on his
death. According to the will, which Connors had witnessed
and Grant had talked about. Both he and Claxby had seen this
as Connors's effort to make Fay's inheritance seem less significant. Which, of course, it had been.

"Have you met her husband?" Meg asked. "Was he at the
seminar?"

"Oh, yes," Maybridge said. "Trevor Martin was there, all
right. A very ordinary, forgettable type. A schoolmaster. Tried
to dispose of his fictional bodies in acid baths but didn't know
his chemistry."

Barker's assessment during the handwriting analysis came
back to him. "If he wanted to dispose of a body, a living body
. . . he'd make sure he knew what he was doing." What else
had he said about him? Not much, but enough to draw the
picture. Extreme discontent.

Maybridge poured himself another glass of liqueur, trying
to remember.

Discontent could kick people into action. The night Grant
had died, Martin had been roaming around—getting milk in
the kitchen, so he'd said, walking in on Major Haydon. It must
have given him a shock seeing Haydon there. So he'd admitted

he'd been up. He'd made a point of coming over to Claxby and himself that day in the canteen. He'd told them before Haydon could. And at the same time had thrown suspicion on Haydon. Nice work. Carefully calculated.

But Grant had committed suicide and with compelling cause. Why doubt it?

"You didn't offer me a drink," Meg complained. "When your policeman's mind begins to work, you forget I'm around."

"Sorry," he said, reaching for her glass.

He had filled it too full, and she took a few careful sips before telling him what she thought he wanted to know. "They seemed an affectionate family—Trevor Martin and his new wife and stepdaughters. The four of them were waiting by the ski lift yesterday. Gina's about my age—well, not far off. Plump. Pleasant looking. Tints her hair auburn. The girls have long fair plaits. They'll be quite something in a few years. They take after their father. Grant was handsome—so you said. And you're right when you say Martin's forgettable. I wouldn't have noticed him if he hadn't been with the other three. They were teasing him about staying on the nursery slopes. It's his first attempt at skiing, I'd guess. He's just a shade more courageous than you. You don't do it at all."

Maybridge asked Meg if she had been introduced to them as Mrs. Maybridge.

"No, nobody was being introduced to anybody. I just happened to be with a few skiing friends, and some of them knew Gina had been married to Grant, and later they talked about it. And don't worry; I didn't contribute to the conversation. Whatever happened at that seminar is over and done with."

She realized that she had been speaking of Gina as if she were still alive. The family of yesterday was strongly in focus —a bright, cheerful group. Then the shadow of today, momentarily forgotten, returned. There was sadness in her voice as she went on. "According to what I heard, she'd tried one of the more difficult runs, lost control, went in the wrong direc-

tion, and smashed into a clump of trees. There were about half
a dozen skiers watching. It must have been horrific. They
couldn't do a thing about it."

"And her husband?" Maybridge asked. "Were was he?"

"Down on the nursery slopes, poor man."

Accidental death, Maybridge decided. He allowed his suspect to walk out of the black tunnel and into the light. Well,
twilight. "Was he there on his own?"

"God give me patience." Meg was truly annoyed. "On the
nursery slopes with about fifty others. And if ever a man needs
sympathy and understanding, that man needs it now."

She was right, of course. The job was twisting him.

Later that evening, while he and Meg were having coffee
in the hotel reception area-*cum*-lounge, Trevor Martin walked
in with his stepdaughters. One of them had tucked her arm
through his; the other was walking a little ahead. All three
were dressed in bright holiday clothes—the girls in yellow
woollies with matching denims, Martin in a royal-blue skiing
outfit. At first glance, they fitted the scene, and then it became
obvious that they were a group apart. Maybridge had a strong
impression of unity. In their grief, they were closely protective
of each other. The one in front stopped and said something.
Martin put his hand on her wrist and rubbed it gently. They
spoke for a few minutes, and then the girls went over to the
lift. Martin hesitated as if unsure what to do. He went to the
desk and spoke to the receptionist, then went through to
the bar.

"There's your opportunity," Meg said. "Go and have a word
with him. I'll take the lift up with the girls. Try and help
thém if I can." The lift wasn't self-operated, and the elderly
operator was waiting for a full load. He held the doors for Meg
while Maybridge waited until she was inside.

He didn't want to follow Trevor Martin; doing the decent
thing in this particular instance was extraordinarily difficult.

A couple of minutes later, they met in the doorway of the bar as Trevor Martin was coming out.

"I thought I saw you," Martin said.

Gina had been dead nine hours. He had spent part of the afternoon in the mortuary and could still smell it, still hear the ring of his footsteps on the tiled floor. Everything outside was unreal, including this big, noisy hotel. He felt as if he were up on a stage in a strong spotlight and that a prompter behind the scenes was feeding his brain with dialogue. He indicated the sofa that Maybridge had just vacated. "Let's sit?" He led the way over. "Were you drinking coffee?" He had noticed the two empty cups. "Shall we order more?" The questions were sharp and clipped. Automatic.

Maybridge nodded. "Please." A spate of nervous talk, a need for action, wasn't unusual in times of stress. He remembered the varied reactions of the writers when they'd been interrogated at the seminar.

They sat down, and Martin called the waiter over. "Two Turkish coffees—one without sugar. *Bez šećera.*"

The waiter repeated *"Bez šećera,"* giving it the right pronunciation, and then said in perfect English, "Sugar for one."

Martin watched him go and then began talking again— about the general standard of service, the food, the wine. What did Maybridge think of the local drinks? Ljuta was even stronger than Šlijivovica—had he tried it yet? Maybridge, wondering how he could stop the flow and launch into a speech of condolence, said he preferred beer.

"My stepdaughters like that revolting raspberry drink Malina and a concoction made from maize and vanilla called Boza," Martin prattled on. "My wife is a wine drinker—was. I mean, she—" The dialogue was going wrong. His thoughts were surfacing through the dark waters into a net of words, and the net couldn't hold them back.

He turned sideways on the sofa and looked at Maybridge.

His eyes, pale blue and bloodshot, were luminous with tears. Maybridge read the question in them. *Why the hell did you come?*

Martin then asked it aloud, "Are you here professionally, chief inspector?"

Maybridge, his previous suspicions alerted again, said he was on holiday.

"It's a coincidence that I should be here, too," Martin persisted. "It isn't one of the large popular resorts. What made you choose it?"

Maybridge explained about Barker's booklet. "He was the handwriting expert who analyzed the handwriting samples at the seminar."

If the speech of condolence wasn't made quickly, it would be difficult to make at all. "I was extremely sorry," he began quietly, "to hear of your wife's accident."

Martin didn't answer. His mind was in a turmoil. Gina had broken herself against a tree. Her skull was smashed. Words. Facts. Not to be looked at. Not to be thought about. This time yesterday they had been dancing together—the kolo—at a Yugoslav knees-up at a hotel down the road. She had pulled him into the dance with her, teasing him out of his shyness.

He hadn't known then that Maybridge was here.

He hadn't known until he had glanced at the hotel visitors' book while they were at the desk waiting for the bedroom key.

Maybridge's sympathy was honest, and he expressed it gently. "It's an appalling tragedy. If there's anything I or my wife can do—"

"There's nothing anybody can do," Martin said. It sounded very matter-of-fact. Even cold.

When they had gone up to their room last night, she had sensed his fear but not understood it. He had told her that they would have to cut the holiday short and go. His excuses were unbelievable. She hadn't known what he was talking about. As the night wore on and his resistance to her questions weakened, she had begun to understand. He would remember the way she had looked at him then. He would remember it forever.

"Was she an experienced skier?" Maybridge asked.

"You'd probably call her average." *She killed herself, policeman. I wasn't there.*

The Turkish coffee arrived, and the waiter indicated the one without sugar. Trevor Martin took it, signed the check, and added a tip.

The tip, Maybridge noticed, was disproportionately large. Either Martin didn't understand the currency or was too troubled to care. The waiter thanked him profusely and then left at some speed.

The coffee was black and tasted very bitter. Maybridge stirred his until all the sugar had dissolved. Martin used a sweetener. Another diabetic? Maybridge wondered. Certainly not a weight problem; he was as thin as a whippet. He probed: "Why those?"

Martin parried: "It's undrinkable without."

A group of young tourists dressed in the colors of a peacock and with voices as raucous came out of the lift and made for the bar. Maybridge looked at them in irritation. This sort of conversation should be taking place somewhere else—somewhere quiet and more private.

He asked Martin when he thought he'd be able to return to England. Martin shrugged. "I don't know. There'll be—" he couldn't think of the right word—"formalities . . . Gina . . . getting her back home . . . the arrangements at the airport . . ."

He let the sentence trail off and began blocking out the horror with another spate of words. "She was so keen to come here. It was the first family holiday for the four of us. We arranged it for a time when the girls weren't in school. They attend a day school in Bath. When we married, I went to live in Gina's home there. It's in one of the Georgian crescents. My own place was south of Bristol in the Barrow area. What

the estate agents call a character cottage. She thought it was
charming but isolated and too small for the four of us. And
too far for the girls to travel to school. So I sold it."

He noticed Maybridge's expression and stopped abruptly.
*And exchanged a run-down property for one worth over a
hundred thousand; that's what you're thinking, isn't it?*

Maybridge was. He wondered where the conversation was
leading and decided to guide it. "Are you still within commut-
ing distance of your school?"

"I could be. But I chose not to be. I find that private tutor-
ing fits in better with my writing." *Financed by Gina's money;
you're thinking that, too.*

It would have been trite and tangential to ask him about his
books, so Maybridge didn't. He wondered, What next? And
waited.

"Gina was lonely after the divorce," Martin went on. "She
divorced Grant when he deserted her for Fay, but of course
you know that. You probably have dossiers on the lot of us
after the seminar." He grimaced bitterly. "I've been self-
sufficient most of my life. Perhaps that's why marriage didn't
attract me when my contemporaries were getting hitched.
But I felt differently when I met Gina. We met three years
ago at a dinner party given by a mutual friend." *And we
needed each other. I need her now. I can't, I won't believe it.*

The events of the night were with him again. He couldn't
block them out. They had slept very little. Gina had got up
early and taken a walk—and refused to let him go with her.
She had appeared very pale and controlled at the breakfast
table and had insisted that they should go to the ski slopes as
usual. The girls, sensing her mood, had been troubled. She
had cared about them. For their sakes, she wouldn't have
killed herself deliberately. It had happened because of her
state of mind. She had been too distressed to take care.

And he was too distressed to care anymore about anything.

The compulsion to talk was dangerous, but he couldn't help himself.

There was a small mosaic pattern on the coffee table, and his fingers traced the brown-bronze outlines as he spoke. "We married a few months ago—shortly after Grant died. Had we married during his lifetime, she would have lost her allowance. Marriage on my salary alone, after what she was used to, wouldn't have been fair to her. Or the girls. I couldn't have afforded the upkeep of the house in Bath. There were several practical reasons to wait. We saw each other on weekends, and we took holidays together. But we wanted more than that. These last few months have been the happiest I've ever known, and she felt the same."

And then you came. And if you're not here professionally, who or what sent you? Nemesis?

There were times when Maybridge disliked his job intensely. Times like this. A few noncommittal words now would block what he sensed was coming. A reassurance that he was indeed on holiday, a few genuine words of compassion to a man who genuinely grieved, a tactful departure. It was certainly tempting.

But Maybridge stayed sitting, saying nothing.

"During the whole of this conversation," Martin went on, "I've told you nothing you don't already know. And what you don't know, you've surmised. I could have avoided you this evening. I could have taken a walk out there on my own and not come back. But I haven't that sort of courage—or cowardice." He looked around the bright, brash hotel room with unseeing eyes. The compulsion to speak was like a strong rope pulling him to an abyss, but at the end of it there might at last be peace. "As I'm sure you rightly guessed just now, I'm diabetic—like Grant. Or perhaps you already knew. I have access to insulin and understand the varying strengths.

"After what happened to Christopher Haydon, Grant might

have killed himself. Had I done nothing, he might have died, anyway, though that thought certainly hasn't consoled me. I changed the vial on the morning of the seminar while Grant was in his office. During the evening, just after the presentation, I walked down the corridor and noticed that his bedroom door was open and the light was on. Fay was tidying up. I just had time to see that she'd put Grant's insulin and syringe on the shelf over the basin. Earlier they had been in his overnight bag, and I'd worn gloves when I handled them. It worried me that Fay's fingerprints might implicate her. Nobody—apart from myself—is implicated in this. Gina knew nothing. She was distressed to learn of Grant's death. He'd treated her badly, but she still had some feeling for him. She was sick with shock when I told her the truth about it last night."

The words came out painfully. His face felt stiff, his mouth thick and bruised. "Most of this you must have known, or you wouldn't be here. She would never have known the truth if you hadn't come."

Maybridge's sympathy suddenly left him like the snapping off of a light. He tried to keep his voice level. "My coming here was purely fortuitous. I—my colleagues and I—were obviously lax in our investigation. We overlooked you." His anger abated a little. "I'm genuinely sorry about the death of your wife, but it has nothing to do with me. You killed Grant. Yours is the responsibility. Your conscience—or fear —made you admit this to your wife after you found out that I was staying in the hotel. I'm not responsible for your conscience, your actions, or the consequences of those actions. You've deprived your stepdaughters of their father. When you came in with them a short while ago, I could sense their affection for you. How do you suppose they'll feel when they know the truth about you? Your conscience is your business, but if it still exists, then for God's sake think about them."

He could see by Martin's expression that the words had

thrust deeply. There had been affection on both sides. "As soon as the formalities here are over," Maybridge told him, "I'll arrange my flight back to England so that I can travel with you. Grant's daughters needn't be told anything yet. My wife will do what she can for them until you get them home."

Martin forced himself to think beyond the present moment. The switch Maybridge had made, probably not deliberately, from "your stepdaughters" to "Grant's daughters" underlined the loosening of ties. The awful solitariness had begun.

He asked Maybridge if the official statement would be made at police headquarters after arriving in England.

"Yes, at Bristol, I'd imagine."

And if you don't make it, Maybridge thought bitterly, there probably won't be a case. With Grant cremated, there might not be enough evidence. So even if it does come to court and you have a good barrister, you might get off. Only a confession can put you inside.

It was necessary to put a call through to Bristol and make a report. Claxby mightn't be there at this hour—nine-thirty here; ten-thirty in England—but another senior officer would take the reins, and it would be unwise to wait until tomorrow. After the fiasco of the seminar, he was doing everything rigidly by the book.

Before leaving to phone, he stood and looked down at Martin. In all his dealings with murderers in the past, there had never been this degree of personal involvement. The words that Cora Larsbury had cut out about solving the murder were all too familiar to both of them. And now that it had been solved, belatedly, there was no joy in it. There seldom was.